N.E. McMORRAN

MOOJAG

and the LOST MEMORIES

Illustrations Kyra-Sky Foster

SPONDYLUXPRESS

First published October 2023 in the UK by Spondylux Press.
Spondylux Press is an independent neurodivergent publisher
set up and run by autists to publish inclusive, own-voice works.

Writing © N.E. McMorran 2023
Editors: Catalina Gutierrez, Tango Batelli
Cover design & layout © Spondylux Press 2023
Cover art & illustrations by Kyra-Sky Foster 2023
Illustration on Page 10 by Chiaki Kamikawa 2020

All rights reserved.

No part of this publication (in any format) may be reproduced, stored
in a retrieval system, or transmitted in any form or by any means,
electronic, mechanical, photocopying, recording or otherwise without
prior written permission from the author / Spondylux Press.

ISBN: 978-1-8380978-8-2 (Print)
ISBN: 978-1-8380978-9-9 (E-book)
ISBN: 978-1-8380978-2-0 (Audiobook
'Moojag and the Auticode Secret')

A CIP catalogue record for this title is available from the British Library.

Printed and bound in the UK by Clays Ltd, using sustainably sourced,
manufactured and FSC certified paper.

Praise for 'Moojag and the Lost Memories'	4
Letter from the Author	6
Dedication	9
Prologue	10
THE WARD	15
WRINKLY OLD BONES	22
PIE	32
RETURN TO THE FACTORY	41
IF YOU DON'T USE IT, YOU LOSE IT	47
PIE GIRLS	57
CONQIP CATCHES A FISH	60
FINDING MONZI	67
IF	73
WRINKLY WRANGLERS	81
MP MARSHMALLOW	86
A TASTE OF YOUR OWN MEDICINE	93
THREE BAD WOLVES	101
REAL ALDON	110
THE AWARD	116
PINEAPPLE DROPS	124
DEJA'S PINEAPPLE	130
THE ZIZANTH, AND A TASTE OF ALDON'S OWN PIE	136
THE TOXIC HALF	144
ISAAC	152
EXOPOF	158
THE BOMB	166
PEACE GAJOOM	174
BOMBSENSE	182
HONEYSUCKLE	188
Sketch your future tech inventions...	202

PRAISE FOR MOOJAG AND THE LOST MEMORIES

PATIENCE AGBABI
Author, *The Leap Cycle*

'Fantastical fun with a deep message about the value of human memories. I loved that the three grannies took centre stage with so much dynamism, humour and wisdom whilst taking memory loss head on. Go grannies!'

ALLIE MASON
Author, *The Autistic Guide to Adventure*

'Fast-paced and action-packed, with more plot twists than you can shake a Gajoomstik at, Lost Memories will keep you guessing until the very last page!'

EMILY KATY
Autism advocate, blogger, author

'Delve back into the magnificent fantasy world of Moojag with this standalone sequel full of joy, and explore what it means to be different.'

DANIEL AUBREY
Author, *Dark Island*

'A fantastic adventure with an important message and authentic and exciting neurodivergent characters. I loved it!'

PRAISE FOR MOOJAG AND THE LOST MEMORIES

ALEX FALASE-KOYA
Author, *Marv / The Breakfast Club Adventures*

'*A captivating adventure... with really fun and whimsical pieces of technology, but still there is a real sense of peril... I have never been so scared of a marshmallow chamber! Most of all though, I love how it pushes back on the idea of older people being useless, not by erasing the things they may find difficult, but by highlighting their strengths... The things they still remember end up being as important as the things they have forgotten.*'

READERS' FAVORITE
5 Star Review by Pikasho Deka

'*An imaginative futuristic adventure that draws you in and keeps you hooked. But it's the characters who win your heart... Vivid, vibrant, compelling, laugh out loud.*'

BEN DAVIS
Author, *Lenny Lemmon*

'*A thrilling adventure with a memorable cast of characters!*'

SEAN FLETCHER
Journalist / Presenter

'*A brilliant story... Positive autism representation with loads of fantastic ideas that take you to another world!*'

Letter from the author

Did you know that, in 2021, my first novel 'Moojag and the Auticode Secret' won the Nautilus Book Award? Well, since then I've been busy editing other books and writing this sequel, as well as looking after my invincible ninety-nine year young gran who inspired it. Sadly, she passed a few months before this book was published. But she did get to see the cover, and had a good giggle at the grannies. She had dementia, which meant she often forgot where she was, which decade she was in, and even who I am. But she was always super positive and brave, and we laughed together a lot, especially because I was going through peri-menopause at the same time, something which adults experience when their bodies start changing again. It's sort of like puberty, but the reverse, and that can make you feel topsy-turvy and forget things too! Even Ben, our dog who's now ten years old—sixty in dog years—has gotten forgetful and a bit blind. Maybe he has a case of dog-o-paws, since he's forever walking into things, while I'm always losing my glasses, and the both of us are constantly trying to remember where we were going! Gran, Ben and I made quite the team. :)

So, use what you've got, because you might not always have it, and there's no guarantee you'll get PIE in 2044! Unless you're a scientist or designer, like Gran in the story, and decide to invent your own... I've left some blank pages at the back of this book especially for you to sketch your own future tech inventions! We're excited to see what bright ideas you come up with—so, if you like, send us a photo and we'll share your work on MOOJAG's website and all over *whatsnapchatinstatwitface*...

Enjoy 'Moojag and the Lost Memories'!

@nemcmorran
@MOOJAGbook
info@moojag.com
www.moojag.com

Photo © *Giota Panagiotou* 2023

For the ones lost to lockdown

Thank you Tessi, for inspiring me with your superhuman positivity; Mum and Maria, for all the reading; editors, Cat and Tango; artist, Kyra-Sky; and everyone who has supported and reviewed the Lost Memories.

This is the sequel to 'Moojag and the Auticode Secret'…

Ten years ago, in 2044, when I was only three, a gigantic tidal wave swept Britain. The 'Great Surge' sunk even more of England, after years of flooding, and turned its highest points into lots of smaller islands. London became London Tops and the Surrey Hills became Surrey Isles. When it got too difficult living on Hampstead Top, without enough land to grow real food, we moved to Box Hill Island in the Surrey Isles. We'd lost Mum and my brother Monzi already, so it was just me, Dad, and Gran. They created the 'Real World': a community of neurodivergents—people who think and feel things differently—living outdoors with the help of our PIEs and 3D printers.

"What are PIEs?" I hear you ask? No, pre-Surgers, they're not stuffed pastries! Before Gran founded the Real World, she invented our amazing solar-charged, full-body electronic skin, complete with a single Spondylux shell device. PIE is the computer we wear instead of clothes to protect us from all weathers and keep us safe from harm and disease. It does everything all your devices can do, too, like *whatsnapchatinstatwitface*. And it has some other incredible functions as well, that I still have no clue about!

We've been living the perfect life, free to be our true selves, ever since. Well, until Adam, Izzy, and I met Moojag, that is! Everything changed again when the outsider led us to Gajoomdom—a curious, sticky, underground world full of artificial sweets, inhabited by the Conqip group (a gang of nasty, smelly, greedy, controlling men); the Pofs (a race of small but super strong winged kids); the Auts (twenty-one autistic coders with super senses); and a bunch of Gajoomstiks (innocent candy-producing robots).

That's as much as I can tell you without spoiling the last story. If you read the 'Auticode Secret', you can find out everything that happened before in Gajoomdom. Or you might lose track of time—like the wrinkly new characters in this story! There's also an audiobook version of the 'Auticode Secret', with an amazing cast of neurodivergent voice actors including narrators Indica Watson and Ria Lina. Or, you could be a rebel like Gran and read this cool adventure first!…

1

THE WARD

Back down in Gajoomdoom with Moojag, I glance up at the fake red-veined blue sky. The painted ceiling is now laced with ever more dried-up candyfloss splotches.

"Did you hear her?" he asks, adjusting his top hat and tidying his tailcoat jacket.

A whiff of liquorice hits my nose as I bend down beside the little violet-flowered bushes to collect the pineapple and my friends' sparkling e-skins. "Who?"

"Mum," he says, pulling me up and spinning us round. "She's here," he adds, skipping off down the criss-cross paved candy path, "underground in Gajoomdom!"

"She's gone, Moojag," I whisper loudly, chasing after him for Conqip Hall. "It was only the ghost of Mum."

He huffs and shakes his head. "Don't believe in

ghosts."

"I heard her, too, but—"

"You see!—"

"It wasn't real. It was just the memory of her; our senses playing tricks—"

"Gibberish," mutters Moojag, stalling in front of the giant, human-sized drainpipe and crossing his arms.

I stop beside him and shrug my shoulders. "She'll always be with us, in spirit—"

"Mumbo jumbo."

I can't force him to believe it, and I can't exactly prove it, either. "Where is she, then?"

He shakes his head. "I *will* find her," he says, taking a bite of the mini sponge cake I gifted him. "Happy *Un*-birthday to you," he mumbles, hovering off the ground to swipe the pineapple from my arm and drop it into his top hat. The weight of the spiky fruit pulls it down, and him along with it, when the sound of tipsy men's laughter echoes through the drain. Their gruff voices fly out the end along with the scent of alcohol, mouldy cheese, and lime pie. Conqips on their way! The stinking green sound skims our eyes, ears, and noses as we sprint across to Conqip Hall and creep in through the thick wooden double doors.

Following after Moojag down the darkened hallway, I trace the wallpaper's coarse ridges with my fingertips. My stomach churns at the smell of roasted meats and sour-apple candy, still lingering in the Conqips' dining room. A shard of light reflecting off one of the framed portraits lights up a stuffed deer's head. I edge away from the wall and catch up to my brother as he turns left, down a small corridor.

THUD, THUD, goes the ground, shaking under my feet as my e-skin soles start to inflate.

THUD, THUD...

I turn to peek back round the corner and gasp at a gang of drunken suited Conqips charging into the hall.

THUD, THUD, THUD...

Moojag pulls me back round after him into a room on the left and softly closes the door behind us. The wall is cold and damp. The air, musty, like pre-Surge old socks and something else.

I know that scent... Izzy—when she was little and wouldn't wear PIE! It's *unpurified* pee! This pee smells funky, though.

"Aldon, is that you?" croaks a weak-sounding,

older female voice. I tap Moojag's shoulder, but he brushes my hand away and hovers over to the woman. He says something but she just hisses at him and shouts, "Who are you? Get out!"

"Moojag," he answers, leaping back.

She giggles. "But you're old enough to be his father!" His father? ...Dad? She's quiet for a moment, then looks him up and down and smiles. "Jack, dear! Have you been back long? Where are you staying?"

"Yes, of course. I'm here every day, *tous les jours*. But I am Moojag, not Jack."

The woman definitely thinks he's Dad. But who's *she*? She sounds a lot like Gran. It couldn't be. Could it? She scans the room and peers back at him. "Is that you, Monzi?" He nods, glancing back at my wide eyes with his. Only Gran could know his birth name—Monzi! Is he thinking she's Gran, too? "Take care! There are strange men and curious small girls with wings who bring us pills we don't need. Are they friends of yours?" She must be talking about the nasty Conqip and their poor brainwashed little Pofs.

"Not exactly, but I am not Monzi, not any more.

I am Moojag. And here is—"

"I'm terribly tired," she says, with a worn-out sigh. "I shall sleep now. It was kind of you to visit. Do come again. You *will* come again, won't you?"

"I live here, too," huffs my brother, glancing back at the sound of big footsteps approaching outside.

"I *know*, dear," she mutters. "Goodnight, Jack." I'm not sure she does know. At least, she keeps forgetting who he is.

"TRAVIS!" yells an older man's voice from the hallway. "Stop gazing at your insipid reflection and open the door!" That sounds a lot like nasty old Conqip leader Aldon!

Moojag grabs my hand and pulls me over to the metal-framed bed. "Under here," he whispers. I crawl beneath it and hide behind the coattails of his jacket, tucking Izzy and Adam's e-skins neatly beside me. I whisper "PIE off," and my skin fades to grey, just as the door handle turns and two men wearing tuxedos stride in.

"I don't know why you bother looking at yourself in the mirror, Travis," says Aldon, brow raised. "You look just as awful as you did this morning."

Travis, Aldon's number III, snorts and combs his

fingers through his pathetic thinned quiff. "Smells like… ooooh, I don't quite know," he says, sniffing the putrid air. "What does it smell of to you, A'?"

"Well, T'," answers Aldon with a disapproving sigh, "let's see if I can help put your finger on it. Could it be the scent of three double-crossing, waste of space Wrinkly Old Bones, who can't remember a thing. *Hmm*?" Travis roars with laughter, snorting even louder as he leans back and almost topples over.

Brix, Aldon's number II, charges in through the lit-up doorway, gasping for breath. He adjusts his bow tie and wipes the dripping sweat from his forehead. "Just spotted Biermont running into Stikleby Hall!"

"What's the reprobate playing at," says Aldon, "disappearing and reappearing on us all the time? Why didn't you reprimand the useless Conqip!"

"Perhaps we shouldn't mind *him*," Brix answers, sticking his neck out and pointing in my direction. I hold my breath as he pulls his sleeves up and swaggers over. "What about *this* one!"

2

WRINKLY OLD BONES

"Moojag!" shouts Brix, eyes glaring. "What are *you* doing in here?" The man's feet, dressed in patent black shoes, step forward, inches from my dulled-silver hands. "I'm quite certain," he continues, turning to Aldon, "you instructed IT to get LOST."

My brother hesitates, trying to find the words on the tip of his tongue. Not on his tongue, obviously, just parked there in his mind waiting to be seen.

"Mother, is that you?" asks the woman.

Aldon rolls back his shoulders, sticks out his chest, and lurches forward to jab the bed with his walking stick. It hits Moojag's coat and skims my shoulder. "Of course not," he replies, in a ridiculously deep voice, "stupid old Wrinkly Bones One."

There's snivelling behind me. I peek round. It's coming from a bed beside this one. There's a third bed behind it.

"Where am I?" sobs another old, but softer, female voice. Strange accent. Mix of English with something else. I can't ask Spondylux—the holograph would light up the entire room!

"Oh, shut up, Wrinkly Bones Two!" shouts Brix.

"I want to go home! NOW," a third old voice calls out from the furthest bed. Deeper than the other two. Highgate Top accent, without a doubt. What Dad says people called 'posh'. Maybe not a woman, though? Their feet dangle off the side of the bed. Roughened soles and unkempt jagged toenails embedded with dirt. "Get me out of this thing!" they demand, grabbing at the raised bed rail. "I want to WALK."

"Have you forgotten, *again*, Wrinkly Bones Three, that you *cannot* walk."

"Golly," says Brix, "has she now become as stupid as she is lazy?"

"It's *they*, not *she*," Highgate Top Posh answers sternly.

"*She* only has *her*self to blame," says Aldon, jabbing

his stick. "Lying around all day like a dead dodo. And then *we* are left with the burden of looking after *her*."

"*They, their, them*," insists Posh.

"No one else would have bothered with *her*," says Brix.

"It's for your own safety, *lady*," chirps Travis, with a hideous smirk.

"As long as you rest up and keep taking your MPs," says Aldon, handing them each a round blue pill pinched between his forefinger and thumb, "you may remember how to walk again, and go wherever you please."

"I *can* walk," insists Posh, sneering at him. They kick their legs up in the air, ready to flip out of bed.

"ZIP YOUR LIP," shouts Aldon. He shoves Travis forward and gags as the Conqip throws Posh's spicy, calloused feet and spindly legs back down. Brix covers them with the blanket and tucks it securely under the mattress. "Until then," Aldon continues, "do as the Pofs tell you, and you will remain safe. But beware—strangers now lurk in Gajoomdom. Grave danger lies outside these four walls." He turns for the door. "Should you make contact with *any* Real Worlder, you *will* report it—IMMEDIATELY."

"Err, sorry," utters Wrinkly Bones Two, cupping a hand to her ear, "what was that you said, dear?"

"Tell on the nerdy Real Worlders," Brix shouts into the startled woman's face, "or you'll never see the light of day!"

"Literally!" calls back Travis, choking on a sugared ring doughnut before spitting a soggy morsel of it onto the floor.

"Wendy Pof sent me—" Moojag spouts out of nowhere (well, obviously *somewhere*. You can't just spout from nothing or nowhere). Aldon glares back, shaking his head, as Brix cackles and sticks out a leg to kick Moojag in the shin. I'm ready to punch the foot away but my brother lifts his leg in time and Brix misses. "—to check on the Wrinklies," Moojag explains, at last. That's right, brother. *Takiwatanga*—in your own time and space.

"Back to Pof Palace, Aut-Pof," calls Aldon. "And STAY there, this time."

Moojag nudges me with his heel and curtseys in super slow motion. Time to move! I tug his coat, so he knows I'm off, and crawl slowly backward until safely under WB2's bed.

"Are you from the eighteenth century, Aut-Pof!" Aldon calls back from the doorway. Moojag stops in his tracks to cover his ears from the other Conqips' jeering. "Go on, just get out." He straightens his jacket and tiptoes past them, glancing back with a wink meant for me, before finally hovering into the corridor. Travis stuffs the remaining third of the doughnut back into his trouser pocket and waltzes out with Brix after Aldon, slamming the door shut behind them.

"It's okay," I whisper, clambering out. Everyone gasps. "It's only me—"

"Zoe!" says the one who thought Moojag was Dad, and now thinks I'm Zoe—Mum? I grip the bed rail to pull myself up, and the woman pokes my Spondylux. She grins at my e-skin lighting up silver. Its hexagonal cells sparkle in the dim light.

The gentle woman in the next bed—WB2—chuckles. I point Spondylux in her direction and whisper "Identify accent". The cute creases at the corner of her eyes fold up like miniature pre-Surge window blinds.

"Lovely glowy skin," she says, inspecting my face. "Just like our little Izzy's." Izzy? How does she know Izzy! I gaze up at the green holographic letters Spondylux has projected over her head:

KENYAN BRITISH

Izzy said her gran was living in Kenya!

"What's your name dear?"

"Nema."

She turns to WB1. "Like you, Nem Avti!"

I gaze at the woman with my name and aim my Spondylux at her. Is it really you…"Gran?"

"Pardon? I'm not old enough to be a gran," she says, giggling. Spondylux scans her body, from the tip of her smooth, wavy, silver hair to the grizzly toes peeking out the end of her grey blanket. "I just had my *eighteenth* birthday, you know!"

Highgate Top Posh howls with laughter, their head of thick, tight, grey-black curls bouncing up and down. "You *wish*, Nem Avti."

Spondylux projects a hologram of Gran. A younger-looking one: the one I remember leaving for Switzerland, then disappearing altogether.

"It really *is* you." I lean in for a hug. "But you look different."

"Really? I don't *feel* different. Who did you say you

were, again?"

"I'm Nema, your granddaughter. What are you doing here, Gran?"

"What are *you* doing here?" calls Posh.

"I think she's Izzy's friend," pipes up sweet WB2.

"So, Adam's friend too, then," says Posh, sticking their nose in the air.

"Nema?" asks Gran, finally. "My dear Nema?"

"Yes, Gran. We thought you were…"

She looks at me, glossy-eyed, and winks. "I'm not ready to go just yet, darling."

"But what are you all doing down here!"

WB2 glares as though she's spotted me for the first time. "HELP!" she cries, "ALDON! HELP!"

"STRANGER DANGER," yells WB3. I jump back and glance at the door.

"Zoe?" Gran whispers. I turn to her and shake my head. "Zoe, darling, *hurry*, the Zizanth have kidnapped Monzi!"

What? "I'm not Zoe. And Aldon just sent Monzi—I mean, Moojag—back to Pof Palace."

"Sorry, dear, I didn't catch that," says WB2, "*which*

Palace? What's a *Pof*, dear?"

"When's dinner coming!" calls Posh. "I'm starving. Why haven't you brought in our meals? What kind of ten-star resort *is* this, anyway!"

Oh no, what's happening! Why does no one understand anything? I press a finger to my lips. "Gran," I whisper in her ear, "it's me, Nema. It's okay, I'm going to get you out of here—"

"I remember!" she calls, delighted. "You're my sweet friend from Brighton pier. You gave me your last stick of rock candy. Remember? This is a fine hospital, isn't it? Do you like it?"

"*Where* are we?" I ask her.

"London Tops, of course. The hospital shelter. Are you feeling quite okay?"

"I'm fine. But we need to get you away from here!"

"Don't fret, my darling Zoe. Has the worry over Monzi, and the experiments, made you terribly confused? I suppose that's why you're in here, too…"

She thinks I'm Mum again now. Maybe if I just go along with it, and pretend to be Zoe, things will make sense and I might find out what she's doing here. That would be lying, of course, but we don't have much choice right now. I take her bony hand in mine. "You're right, Nem Avti. I think it might really help if you could remind me exactly how I got here. How *we* got here?"

"Of course. Well, as you know, it all started with the *glorious* octopus!"

3

PIE

"Octopus?" I ask, checking the door and turning back to Gran.

"Oh my, you really *have* forgotten," she says. I nod. "Well, it was back in '34. When London Tops was still just London. I was upcycling clothes for the homeless kids at the flood relief shelter. Do you remember that first day we met, Zoe?" If I say no, it'll probably confuse her. I nod. "We talked for hours, didn't we!" She smiles. "Thinking up ways we could create a better world. It was too late to do anything about the climate, of course, but we could still figure out a better way to live in our brave new world. We set about designing the perfect home, where people didn't need money, oil, houses, even doctors, to survive."

"Is that when you came up with PIE?"

"When *we* came up with PIE, dear," says Gran, smiling. "And my boy, too, of course."

Dad? "You mean, Jack?"

"Yes, of course, my Jack. He discovered the trashed bio e-skin research, developed in the twenties for the robots but never used!"

"Why didn't they use it?"

"Well, for one, the skin was virtually unbreakable. But, more importantly," she adds, pinching my arm, "it was self-healing, just like real human skin! Even the electronics inside the bio-material were indestructible. Not like the other devices and robots we used in the twenties."

"And all those apps, too!" I add. Dad said it cost people a fortune just to contact each other. Everyone all thought *whatsnapchatinstatwitface* was free, but they kept needing new devices for the updates. "So, with the digital skin, you wouldn't have had to keep buying new ones?"

"Right. And that's exactly why the big guns running the world quickly put a stop to the research. Big Con realised that everyone would stop buying all their other devices."

"And stop making them loads of pre-Surge money,

too!"

"Quite. Then, of course, I had my brainwave to invent a single computer that people could wear, which would simultaneously do what all the apps did. That would protect us from the weather and monitor our health, too, all at the same time. Something we could actually live in, outdoors forever, and for free!"

"PIE?" I ask, grinning so wide I feel like my face might split.

"The one and only. No need for buildings. No need for medicine. No need for anything, really. Nothing but our own bodies, nature, and PIE. That was when you and Jack travelled all around the world, to work with the incredible scientists behind the octopus-inspired digital skin." Gran raises an arm and swooshes her hand through the air like a plane. "From Texas, Pennsylvania, and Stanford to Athens, Beijing, and Tokyo, and last, but not least, down under to Wollongong!" She pats my shoulder. "You developed the formula together and collected all the materials we needed to finally produce PIE. By the time you came home," she says, giggling and flashing me a wink, "you were *together* together."

I smile.

"Good man," mutters WB2, eyes and nose peeking out from her bed covers like a curious little mouse, "that Jack of yours."

I nod, smiling back.

"Bright kid," WB3 adds, nodding to Gran. "Though not quite as quick as my Isaac…"

Gran frowns and gazes back at me. "You and Jack were inseparable."

"Their idea of a romantic evening," continues WB3, raised brow, "was a lock-in, chatting about motherboards and games. What was that thing you used to say, Nem Avti?"

"'Love at first download'," chuckles WB2, lifting her trembling hands from under the covers to join them in the shape of a heart.

I choke, laughing, and shrug my shoulders. Dad never said how they met. I knew Mum was an engineer too, but he never told me they made PIE together.

"Then," adds Gran, "they made Monzi!"

TMI, Gran. I hope my brother is all right. How'll I get them all out of here, and rescue the Pofs too, without his help? And Gran's brain is at least thirteen years behind.

I have to find out what's going on—*fast*.

"So, how did we end up *here*, Gran?—I mean, Nem Avti."

"*Takiwatanga*, Zoe. Remember, everything in our own time and space."

"Yes, of course. Whenever you're ready."

"Well, let's see… Monzi… err… Yes, he was, mmm, having trouble at…" Gran gazes up at the ceiling and sighs.

"You okay?" I ask, taking her hand.

The door suddenly opens, lighting up the room, and Moojag hovers in. "Jack, is that you?" calls Gran, squinting at him.

"*Non, c'est moi*. Moojag."

"Have you seen my Isaac?" Posh asks. My brother just huffs. "He's coming to see me today," they say, sticking their nose in the air. "We're going out for lunch. A fancy place, of course."

Poor Posh thinks her son Isaac is still alive. But Adam's dad died years ago. And, anyway, I'm pretty sure there aren't any 'fun sea places' round here!

"*Sure*," says Moojag, turning to me with a wink. "Now to the Gajoom soldiers, sister Nema. Quick, quick.

Vite, vite."

"What? What Gajoom soldiers!"

"We didn't catch all the angry Gajooms," he answers, shaking his head. "Biermont and I spotted one with its three moody little clones, just before you came back down here. He's been looking for them and printing more antidote strips to reverse their meanie code!"

If we did miss some angry Gajoomstik robots, then our Real World is *still* in danger. We have to find them quick, and apply the antidote strips, before they multiply even more!

"Are the rock candy robots in trouble?" cries Gran. Waves of her silver-white hair spring about as she jolts upright. "What has that monster done to our Gajoomstiks!"

Three pairs of shining granny eyes fix on me as I explain everything that has happened. I tell the story of how Adam, Izzy, and I met Moojag, then found this place and discovered the Conqips building a Gajoom army to destroy our perfect Real World. About us helping the Aut workers escape, but having to leave all but three Pofs behind.

Moojag drops his jacket to show Gran his wings. "I knew you would reveal them one day, Monzi," she says, tapping her chest with her fist.

"He discovered he was a Pof, as well as an Aut," I say, as all three grans nod back knowingly. "We planted the antidote on the Gajoomstiks, but," I explain, shaking my head, "we must have missed one, and now it's bounding free around Gajoomdom and self-replicating—"

"Aldon will make war with the Real World," adds Moojag, "if we don't stripe the moody Gajoomstiks before he finds them."

"We'd better get our pre-Surge skates on, then!" exclaims Gran, frowning as she prods us both. "But I never want to hear either of you say the W word ever again."

Moojag ponders for a moment, gazing down at his feet. Checking for actual skates? Nope, no skates. He looks back up, disappointed.

"Are you well enough, though?" I ask Gran, bowing my head.

"Of course she is," yells Posh, arms crossed. "Nothing a good meal won't cure. Not a *blue* one, though."

Gran kicks her legs up as Moojag unhinges the bed's safety lock and lowers the rail. He passes her the sponge cake and lets her take a big bite before pulling her forward.

Moojag's cicada muscles bulge under his sleeves as Gran tries to stand. But she wobbles with her knees giving way, and falls back to perch on the edge of the bed. Leaning against my shoulder, she slaps herself in the face like a frustrated robot. The other grans sigh, shaking their heads.

"Thank you for coming, Jack and Zoe," whimpers Gran, head hanging down. "Promise you'll come again." Her eyelids close as Moojag and I lay her back down on the bed. "We'll talk tomorrow…" she mutters, "about the good old days—" and then falls asleep the second her head hits the pillow. Never understood how she does it. Literally can't remember the last time I fell straight to sleep like that. Have I ever?

"Is she alive?" calls WB3, tipping back onto their bed now, too. "Always dropping off, that one."

WB2 chuckles. "No idea what year it is, poor dear. How could anyone forget 2044—year of the Great Surge." Well, at least WB2's only running *ten* years behind. "Goodnight, dear," she says, wiggling her fingers at us. She rolls over and a little fart jets out. A lot like one of Izzy's but much longer, and, luckily, also not smelly.

"Lock door," mutters WB3, half-asleep. "Don't want no meanies creeping in."

4

RETURN TO THE FACTORY

"What happened?" I ask Moojag. "How come they all fell asleep at the same time?"

My brother throws up his arms. "Evil blue pills."

"The little round things Aldon gave them?" I ask. "What are they?"

"Drugs, to help them walk again," he answers, tipping his top hat and pointing to his head. "But Pari Pof says," he whispers in my ear, "they just make them fall asleep, and *forget*, too."

"How long have they been taking them?"

"Every day."

Every day? "How long have they been down here?"

My brother starts to work, his mind ticking away.

"Twenty-four thousand," he announces, "eight hundred and twenty hours."

Wait. "Calculate," I call into Spondylux. "24,820 hours divided by 24 hours. Equals: 1,034 days. Divided by 365 days a year. Equals: two point eight years?"

"*Non*," he answers, pulling the gold smart-watch from his waistcoat pocket and shoving it in my face. "*Thirty-*four hours in a Gajoomdom day, my Real World sister."

Of course. "Calculate 24,820 hours divided by 34 hours. That's 730 days. Divided by 365 days a year. Equals: two RW years?" He nods. "Gran stopped writing to us about two years ago—which means she must have been down here since then!"

Moojag's eyes swing to the side, avoiding mine. "I did not know. How could I!"

"Of course you couldn't, stuck in with the Auts all this time. So, how come they remember some stuff really well, but keep forgetting who we are?"

"Pari said their long term memory flits back and forth, in and out. Sometimes *absolutement* clear! Like time travel, but without moving. You have seen *Back to the Future*?" Only sixty times! I nod. "And the short term memory—*toooooooo* short."

Poor Gran. It must be so scary not being able to remember things she would never have wanted to forget. Like who *we* are. Her own family. Does she forget who *she* is, too?

STIK! goes a thud in the corridor. ***GAJOOOOOM*... STIK!** *GAJOOOOOM*... **STIK!** *GAJOOOOOM*... **STIK!**

Moojag glares at me. "Gajoom and clones. *Vite, vite.*" He gestures for my hand and we make for the door. I glance back at our snoring grannies, laying perfectly still in their beds, and tiptoe out after Moojag.

My PIE skin lights up the way through the dining hall. Past the long wooden antique table and red velvet-covered chairs; the Conqip portraits; the animal heads; Brix's double-decker chaise-longue; a lonely blue crab claw on the floor by the other door. The same door I came through before with Adam and Izzy in our Gajoom disguises.

Moojag peeks out into the long tunnel corridor and signals to his back. He's left his jacket in the Ward. He must feel even braver now, having shown his real self to Gran. I take hold of the wings that look so delicate, yet feel like solid pre-Surge steel, and wrap my legs around his middle.

He hovers up off the ground and ferries us down the corridor. "To the factory," he whispers, "for the Auticode strips."

"Have the missed Gajooms gone back there?"

"*Non*. They bolted to Stikleby Hall for the Conqip Awards." Oh my. Conqip Awards. Prizes the Conqip probably award their nasty selves!

Reaching the end of the corridor, my brother gently sets me down. I release his glowing, effervescent wings and he grins, pressing his hands together before taking a bow. I return his bow with a lower one. He returns mine with an even lower one. You get the idea. Now both our faces are almost touching the floor with our bums in the air. "Come on," he says, springing back up.

Something feels off. Something's missing… I check under my arms. The PIEs! "Moojag," I whisper, scanning the ground. "Adam and Izzy's PIEs. I left them back in the Ward—"

"No time. Liquorice strips to fetch." Moojag presses a finger to his lips. "Wait here." He draws a circle with his arm and I stand with my back to the wall as the round door panel releases and rotates up. He leaps through the window into the factory.

"What the devil are you doing in *here* now, Aut-Pof! Have you lost *all* respect? You insolent little brat."

"*Pardon*, Brix, sir."

"Oh! *Three* words from you, this time, stupid boy. Well done, I suppose. Though one of them isn't even English. You do realise how disgusting you sound?"

Poor Moojag, I'm sure he *feels* disgusting right now, being spoken to like that. I don't get it. To me, he sounds perfectly poetic and unique. It's not easy hearing the sound of your voice, though, is it? I guess, just like me, Moojag can't stand hearing his own voice, either.

"Pofs... need... cake."

"Do... they... now."

"*Oui... oui... oui.*"

"Peed ourselves again, have *we*?"

"Have *you*?"

"COME HERE RIGHT NOW!...

...TAKE THIS and GET OUT, before I summon Travis and we throw you into the Marshmallow Chamber!"

5

IF YOU DON'T USE IT, YOU LOSE IT

I gasp as Moojag leaps back through the porthole, unscathed, carrying a pink frosted muffin topped with purple mini marshmallows. He closes the panel, hauls me up with a single flexed arm, and flies us like a flash of lightning all the way back to the Ward.

"Good morning, Moojag," chirps Gran. "And... girl." At least she remembers *him* this time.

"No breakfast, then?" moans Posh. "The service here is abominable. I demand to see the manager!"

"I love eggs, you know," pipes up WB2, cute little orange freckles popping over her cheeks. "I hope it's eggs and cheese!"

"It's only us, Nema and Moojag," I say. Their smiles turn upside down. "We couldn't get the strips. Brix was in the factory."

"Tips? There *won't* be any tips, girl."

"Who's Brix, dear?" asks Gran, squinting. "Moojag, is that you there? *Bonjour*, my sweet Aut-Pof."

"I love eggs and cheese! I hope it's eggs and cheese."

Moojag hovers over to the door and sticks his ear to it.

"28 hours," a timid, tinny voice calls from outside, making Moojag jump. "Dinner time, ladies." He pushes against the door while I roll under WB2's bed and out of sight. He can barely keep it closed. Whoever it is must be just as strong as he is. He releases the door, letting a petite, violet-winged Pof girl stumble into the room carrying three bowls on a tray with one hand. She brushes back the blonde ringlets covering her eyes and peers at Moojag's waistcoat. He takes out the muffin and passes her half. The little girl pops the whole lot in her mouth as he wipes the pink frosting from his fingers onto the handkerchief hanging from his pocket. It's Pari Pof, Wendy's daughter, still wearing her matching purple t-shirt and shorts. She nods and skips forward, placing the tray on a small folding table at the foot of the first bed. "WB1, soup." She passes a bowl to Gran and moves on to Freckles. "WB2, soup." And finally, "WB3—"

"SOUP?" Posh is livid. "Is this what ten-star service has come to in 2040 Nairobi? Abominable. I *must* see the manager."

Pari turns back and hovers over to Moojag. "I don't like *them*."

"I bet they're perfectly soft on the inside," says my brother. "Just need a spoonful of sugar." Or maybe just a little *love*.

"They need *these*," says Pari, revealing three blue pills cradled in the palm of her cupped hand. She deals them out to the grannies. "Would anyone like a little trot around the room?" she asks.

"Yes, please!" answers WB2, placing her hand on her chest. Pari releases the bed rail, but Freckles shakes her head. She even can't summon the strength to sit up.

"Come on, WB2," says Pari, "you can do it!" She places a hand on Freckles' back to hold her steady, lowers her legs off the bed, and grips her upper arm to help her stand. Freckles' eyes light up as she manages to take a step forward, and another, but then sways to the side.

"I'm going!" she cries, glancing at Pari hovering

beside her. Pari grabs Freckles' arm as she swings back and flops onto the bed.

"You *can* walk, Wrinkly Bones Two," whispers Pari. "One and three, too! I heard Aldon tell his friends." He has friends? "He just keeps them in bed so he doesn't have to care." Pari tugs Moojag's waistcoat. "I've been walking them every day. But Aldon darling told us off and locked them back up in their beds." Pari's small eyes widen. "They've been lying there for so long, I think maybe their bodies have forgotten how to move!"

Gran always used to say, 'If you don't use it, you lose it'.

"She *will* walk again," says Moojag. "*Takiwatanga*—in her own time and space."

Pari hovers round Moojag and swipes his hat. "If you say so," she says, plopping it back on his head and saluting him.

As Moojag helps her collect the empty bowls, the door swings open and another Pof enters, carrying a pile of something. "Pee Pants," calls the winged girl, all dressed in orange. She snatches the other half of the muffin from Moojag's pocket, stuffs it in her tutu pouch, and links arms with Pari. They skip up to the first bed and shove their hands under the small of Gran's back. "Ready..." they call out together, "steady... go!" They heave, rolling her onto her side. Pari drags up Gran's grey nightie and pulls down a sodden, steaming wad of *unpurified* pee. Orange Pof strings it up and waves it in front of poor Gran's face, then lobs it onto the floor, a foot too close to my face. "You wouldn't have to wear a nappy," she says, wrinkling up her nose, "if you weren't so *really, very lazy*."

Pari shakes her head and nudges Orange Pof. "It's a lie! They *can* walk, they've just lost all their power."

"NO," demands the fierce-faced Pof. "Aldon *is* right." She zooms round, yanking the nappies off the other two WBs. "He gave me a *giant* chocolate orange! That's all the proof I need." She picks up three fresh pull-up pants and chucks them at each of the grannies. "Come on, Pari, we can *not* be late for the Awards. Conqip II will confiscate all my orange jelly beans... and you know how I *only* really like orange."

"Okay," says Pari, skipping round the beds to stroke each of the grannies' faces. "Moojag, are you coming?" she asks him, turning for the door. "Aldon's so very cross."

"Moojag fears not the Marshmallow Chamber," says my brother, hands on hips. "He is quite fondant of sinking in the squishy, pink gunk." The Pof girls hover out of the room, flapping their wings at him and slamming the door shut behind them.

"I'm NOT a baby," calls out Posh, throwing down the pull-up pants. Freckles whimpers, trying to stick her feet through the nappy's leg holes.

I climb back out from under the bed to help Gran pull on hers. "I love you," she says, stroking my cheek like I'm a cat. She gazes at me, turns away for a moment, and then looks back. "Are you new? I haven't seen you in here before."

I nod, pulling up the nappy. "I'm your granddaughter, Nema."

She squints at me. "Nema?"

"Yes."

"That's a beautiful name... I'm beautiful, too!"

"She would make a splendid partner for my Jasira," says Posh, fumbling under their covers.

"Maybe Zoe doesn't like girls," suggests Freckles, also fidgeting under her blanket as though she's being tickled.

"I'm Nema."

"Sorry, dear. Of course you are."

"Nonsense," says Gran. "Now, leave Zoe alone. She's confused enough as it is. And anyway, she's with my Jack!"

"Isaac's coming to take me out for luncheon today," says Posh, jerking their head. "Works for Big Con, now, you know. *Very* important position. Only the finest—"

"Ten-star cuisine?" adds Gran. "Yes, you may have mentioned it once or twice."

What's a 'luncheon'? Cool word, though, *luncheon. Luncheon. Luncheon—*

"Luncheon!" exclaims Moojag, turning to me with a grin. I nod, shoulders hunched.

Gran grabs my chest by the e-skin and pulls me in close to whisper in my ear, "I can get you your strips."

"How?"

She pulls her other shaky hand out from under the blanket and presents three round blue pills, cradled in her sweaty, blue-stained palm.

Posh and Freckles throw down their covers and bolt up, wearing Izzy and Adam's e-skins! "There's nothing you

can't do when you have PIE," calls Freckles, bouncing on the bed and clapping her hands.

If only Izzy and Adam could see *this*. Their grannies are so much like them. Or are *they* so much like their grannies?

6

PIE GIRLS

Gran points to my glistening, silver skin, and back at herself. "You don't mind if I borrow that?" She pulls out a nightshirt from under the mattress and hands it to me. "And this will be perfect on you."

"But can you walk, Gran?" I ask, slipping the shirt over my head and stepping out of PIE.

"*We* don't need to walk," calls Posh. "That's PIE's job!"

"What do you mean? PIE can't walk."

Freckles catapults from her bed in Izzy's glowing turquoise skin. She lands softly beside me and pokes my middle with a chuckle. "It's good to be back!"

"You do look very fine, Sophia," says Posh, standing

tall in Adam's sparkling, rainbow-coloured skin.

"Thank you, Stella," replies Sophia, twirling on the spot. "I just adore this blue-green! It's as though I'm wearing the incredible Indian Ocean…"

"How come no one ever told us PIE *moves*?" I ask, glaring wide-eyed at the now unnaturally upright grannies.

"I always told Jack everything," says Gran, pulling the PIE up over her nightie. But Dad never said anything about transport! "The function is strictly for emergency use. I designed PIE to work with us, not *for* us. After all, if you don't use the miracle-of-a-body life gave you—the way we're meant to—you lose it! Game over. *Kaput.*"

Dad had a point, though. We wouldn't have done any exercise—not the natural kind, anyway. Like pre-Surgers driving everywhere when they could easily walk. They even counted 'steps' inside their cement boxes, using *pacbitsweatgoogfitpal* instead of their own brains, or ran on the spot in a gym, instead of out in the crisp, fresh air. They were all 'running nowhere, fast'.

Moojag pulls out his pocket smartwatch. "Next MP dose: twenty minutes, ten seconds, and counting…"

"Now, dear," says Gran, "where do we find these

bricks and strips?"

"The candy factory," I answer. "And it's 'Brix'."

"That's what I said, dear, 'bricks'. And how many strips did we need?"

"*Cinq? Dix? Peut-être plus.*"

"We'll just bring them all," says Gran, squinting at Moojag and clasping his hand to guide him over to the bed. "Now, get in, Monzi, and stay quiet. If we aren't back in time for our pills, remember what I taught you at the clinic." Moojag nods, climbing into the bed. "Sophia, Stella, look after him." They nod, holding up their glowing thumbs, and we leave the Ward: just me in the oversized, pre-Surge nightie and my super shining-silver Gran.

CONQIP CATCHES A FISH

"This is it," I whisper, reaching the factory door with Gran. She crouches down, peels off my PIE skin and hands it back to me. I hold out my arm to point at the wall and draw a wide circle in the air. The round panel pops out and rotates up, letting multi-coloured rays of apple and raspberry light beam through the gap.

"Who's there?" calls a raspy male voice on the other side of the wall. "Present yourself!"

Gran presses a finger to her lips and waves me back. "Help," she calls, whimpering as she sticks her head and arms through the opening.

"WB1? What in the name!"

"Help me, Travis, dear!"

"*Ugh*, how very *dare* you. I'm not that smug, stuck-up snitch."

It sounds like Conqip Brix, with the sour face and repulsed stare.

"Biermont?" she says, meekly. "Is that you?"

An angry arm juts out of the hole, grabbing Gran and pulling her into the factory.

"How on Earth did you get here, woman?"

"The Pofs," she answers. "One of my banoffee cravings, dear. They were in a hurry to get to the Awards, you see, so the little Mights just dropped me here."

"Those dizzy Pofs! Heads all over the place. I *suppose* we could spare you a candy off-cut from the reject pile. This is absolutely the last time, mind. You've bitten off far more than you can chew, wouldn't you say."

What on Earth can he mean? She hasn't bitten off or chewed *anything*.

"...Thank you," answers Gran. "So kind, dear—"

"Just shut up and eat."

"...*Mmm*, delicious."

"Wait here, woman," says Brix, "and don't move an inch... Oh, right, you *can't*," he adds, snickering off into the distance and muttering to himself, "I ought to leave the greedy wench down here when the whole place goes *poof*..."

What does he mean, 'goes *poof*'!?

The Conqip anthem blares from the loudspeaker and a door slams shut. "Zoe!" calls Gran. Zoe? Oh right, yes, that's *me*. I leap in and dash straight past her, through a candyfloss mist, to make for the remaining Auticode strips piled up beside the humongous printer. I haul the entire bundle over to Gran, and help her back into my e-skin. She bolts up with a grin, scoops all the strips together to lay them across her shoulders, and bounds out like a Gajoom. I chase after her all the way back to the Ward.

"Only us," says Gran, sneaking back into the barely-lit room. The other grans cheer from their beds.

"Bravo," says Moojag, leaping out and kneeling beside the mound of sticky strips with his hands pressed together.

"Who are you?" Gran asks him. She's already forgotten him again. "Get out of my room! HELP!"

"HELP!" screams Stella. "Stranger danger!"

Moojag jumps back into Gran's bed and Sophia starts to cry. Only her knobbly, hooked fingers and a

"*Ugh*, how very *dare* you. I'm not that smug, stuck-up snitch."

It sounds like Conqip Brix, with the sour face and repulsed stare.

"Biermont?" she says, meekly. "Is that you?"

An angry arm juts out of the hole, grabbing Gran and pulling her into the factory.

"How on Earth did you get here, woman?"

"The Pofs," she answers. "One of my banoffee cravings, dear. They were in a hurry to get to the Awards, you see, so the little Mights just dropped me here."

"Those dizzy Pofs! Heads all over the place. I *suppose* we could spare you a candy off-cut from the reject pile. This is absolutely the last time, mind. You've bitten off far more than you can chew, wouldn't you say."

What on Earth can he mean? She hasn't bitten off or chewed *anything*.

"...Thank you," answers Gran. "So kind, dear—"

"Just shut up and eat."

"...*Mmm*, delicious."

"Wait here, woman," says Brix, "and don't move an inch... Oh, right, you *can't*," he adds, snickering off into the distance and muttering to himself, "I ought to leave the greedy wench down here when the whole place goes *poof*..."

What does he mean, 'goes *poof*'!?

The Conqip anthem blares from the loudspeaker and a door slams shut. "Zoe!" calls Gran. Zoe? Oh right, yes, that's *me*. I leap in and dash straight past her, through a candyfloss mist, to make for the remaining Auticode strips piled up beside the humongous printer. I haul the entire bundle over to Gran, and help her back into my e-skin. She bolts up with a grin, scoops all the strips together to lay them across her shoulders, and bounds out like a Gajoom. I chase after her all the way back to the Ward.

"Only us," says Gran, sneaking back into the barely-lit room. The other grans cheer from their beds.

"Bravo," says Moojag, leaping out and kneeling beside the mound of sticky strips with his hands pressed together.

"Who are you?" Gran asks him. She's already forgotten him again. "Get out of my room! HELP!"

"HELP!" screams Stella. "Stranger danger!"

Moojag jumps back into Gran's bed and Sophia starts to cry. Only her knobbly, hooked fingers and a

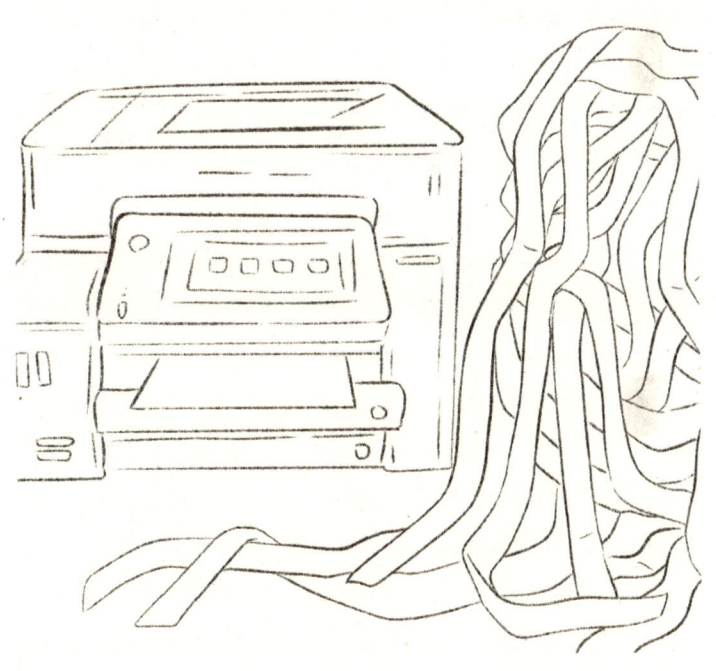

few auburn-silver curls peek out from her bed covers. The Conqip are bound to come running now.

"*C'est moi*—Moojag," whispers my brother.

"We don't care *who* you are," shouts Stella, "get out, before I call the Resource Police!"

They must think it's the Resource Wars. That was in the thirties, before the Surge. When pre-Surgers still lived in cement boxes they called 'houses'. And only a few families still had natural sugar. People would beg for it. Sometimes they'd even break into our cement box to steal it! Dad said he 'would've gladly given it, had they only asked'.

Moojag shakes his head and jumps back out of the bed; Gran climbs in; and I crawl under. He swipes all the strips, stashes them inside a white wardrobe in the corner of the room beside Stella's bed, and climbs in on top of them before closing the door.

"What in heavens is going on, Wrinkly Bones?" calls Travis, striding in. He combs back his limp quiff. "Why aren't you all sleeping, like good old wrinkly girls?"

"There's a MAN in here," calls Gran.

"Yes, ladies. I *am*," he says, sticking his nose in the air, "a MAN." He stands stiff and straight, feet together and hands firmly on his hips.

"Not *you*, Con Boy," calls Stella, pointing down. "The one under there!"

Oh no. I shuffle back as an arm swings for me under the bed.

"Come out, come out... whoever you are!" The mingled scent of sweat and fishy breath bursts into my nostrils as his hand whacks my head and he drags me out by the neck. "What's this?" he says, stringing me up like a prize-winning Frankenfish. "Have I caught myself a Real Worlder?" I choke as he lets go of my throat and grips my shoulder. I glance down at my body dressed in the strange pre-Surge dress. Gran's still wearing PIE! I look back at her, but the hood's pulled down and her blanket is covering the rest of her body. "Why are you wearing Wrinkly Bones One's clothes?" he asks me.

Hmm, what do I say? I could be from somewhere else. I'll tell him I'm not a Real Worlder. I'll say... "I'm from Glasgow!" *Glasgow*?

"Are you quite all right, strange girl?" Not afraid of him. He's just a selfish troll who can't control his sugar intake. Not nearly as mean as Brix. "I think you'd better take an MP," he says, rummaging inside his dinner jacket pocket and pulling out a little blue pill. "This might help you remember. Then we can send you back to your perfect little life, so you can do whatever it is you do, before you lose it, you filthy little dropout." I try to wriggle free, but he's stronger than I ever imagined and now I'm stuck. He cranks my jaws open with his fingers, shoves the pill inside my mouth, and muzzles me with his sticky hand. What did he *mean*, 'before I lose it'? "Swallow!" I hold the pill on my tongue, breathing through the nose, but my mouth fills up with so much spit that I can't help but gulp the pill down with it. Travis finally lets go and I gasp for air. The grans are quiet, eyes glazed over and staring into nothing; at nobody. Travis walks over to Stella's bed, dragging me behind him by the wrist. "You lot can have your pills early today. Quite enough award time has been sacrificed as it is." He hands out the pills and waits, arms crossed, for everyone to swallow, before ordering me into Gran's bed with her. He marches out muttering something about us going '*poof*'! The door slams shut and, from the keyhole, a *clink clunk*.

8

FINDING MONZI

The cupboard door swings open and Moojag tumbles out. "*Mon dieu*, Travis locked the door—"

"Jack, is that you?" asks Gran. "I forgot the avocados. Would you be a darling and fetch me a dozen?" Are there avocados in Gajoomdom? I wonder what decade she thinks we're in now. I look over at the other grans snoring in their beds.

"We don't have real fruit or veg," says Moojag. "This is Gajoomdom."

"Ga-*what*, now?" she asks.

"We're underground."

Her head swivels slowly round and she glares at me, terrified. "Time is running out, Zoe. We must get to the clinic before Aldon, or we'll lose Monzi—forever."

What do I say? Tell her I'm *not* Mum? But that'll upset her even more. "We just need to wait 'til they open the door, Nem Avti," I say, taking her hand in mine under the covers.

"If only we'd come up with PIE sooner," she says, squeezing my fingers hard. "We could've flown in there and grabbed him back. No one any the wiser."

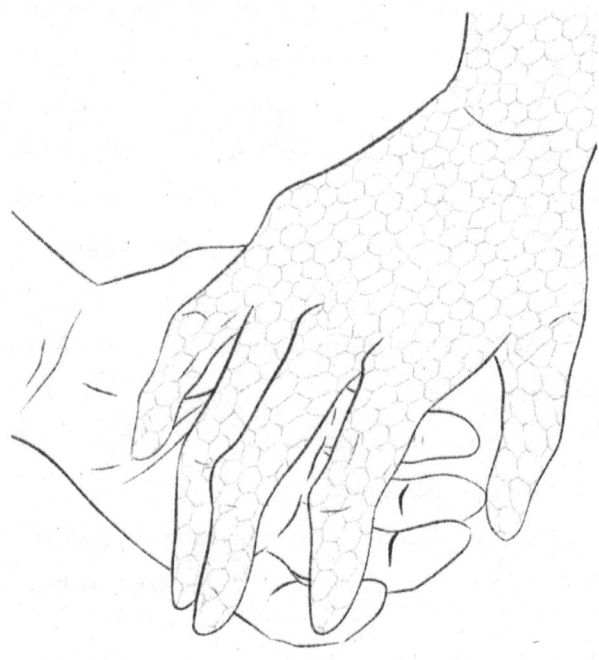

"What do you mean, Nem Avti?"

"The IF, of course," she says, poking me.

"Wait—wasn't Monzi sick? Why would we have to sneak him out?"

"Zoe, dear. Sometimes we just have to block out the bad things that happen to us. To forget. And for some, to deny the bad things they've done."

Did Mum do something awful? What's the IF? "What did I do, Nem Avti?"

"You gave poor Monzi to the Zizanth, didn't you? For the wicked 'cure trials'."

Moojag frowns at me and bows his head. "She thought she was doing right, Nem Avti."

"Well, darling Jack," Gran says, releasing my hand and turning to Moojag, "she had a funny way of showing it, vanishing off the face of the earth like that."

"I'm sorry," I say. Though, it's Mum, really, who should be apologising. But everyone said Monzi was sick. They said he had a virus and couldn't come home. Isn't that what they were trying to cure? Was that when Monzi became a Pof? But Mum died in the Surge. Why is Gran talking like Mum *wanted* to disappear?

"You did what you had to do," she says. "You're back now, that's the important thing."

"Where did I go?" I ask.

"You tell *me*, dear. You were quite lost."

"You mean, I couldn't find my way home in the floods?"

"Not at all. In your head, dear. You had too many worries. I suppose you've just never been able to forgive yourself for what happened to Monzi."

"But Jack told Nema that I died!"

Gran looks round at Moojag and shakes her head. "Well, you shouldn't have done that, dear Jack, but you lost hope. We all did. You needed to move on."

"Is that when you left London Tops," I ask, "for RW?"

"Yes, and it was the right time. Hampstead Top was the last dry Top in London, but there wasn't enough space for everyone. We couldn't survive there any longer without enough clean water or natural food. So we collected all the materials to make enough PIEs for our community, and we chose Surrey Isles to make our new home."

"Why Surrey Isles?"

"You see, when I went to pull Monzi out of that clinic, he wasn't there. I searched everywhere, but the place was abandoned except for lead scientist Charlie Schwing. She told me I was too late: that Big Con had marched in just hours before to take Monzi and all the girls to 'safety'." Gran shakes her head and sighs. "She said they'd offered the parents a deal after persuading them they wouldn't be able to cope with their new super-strong, even more hyperactive, children. That it would be in everyone's best interests if the children were adopted in return for their special abilities. There were others, too: autists like Monzi, with incredible long-term memories and problem solving skills, who had also been adopted months earlier. She was on her way to join them all."

Gran must be talking about the Pofs and the Super Auts!

"Schwing warned me to go home," Gran continues, "but I didn't! I followed her all the way to the lighthouse at Juniper Top in the Surrey Isles. By the time I docked, she had disappeared, just like that. I searched all over, but nothing. I waited through the night, and the next three days—no sign of her, or anyone else. I finally gave up and returned to Hampstead Top. That's when Jack and I decided it was finally time to move. Box Hill Island was the perfect location for our new world, and our last chance of finding Monzi. From there, we could see sixteen nautical miles out to sea and what remained of London Tops. But, most importantly, it was close to the lighthouse..." I want to keep listening but my head is a mess, my arms feel so heavy, and my eyelids can barely stay open. "Zoe, dear, are you all right?" Gran's voice sounds quiet as a mouse now. "It's the MP. She's falling asl..."

9

IF

"WAKE UP!" I jump at the loud, fuming voice vibrating through my ears before my eyes spring open and a man's scheming, scrunched-up face meets mine. I turn away from his stale breath. "So the pathetic 'Real Worlder' had the audacity to come back, eh?" Me? Real Worlder? Who? Wait—where am I? What's happened to my brain? Who is this nightmarishly familiar man? He sniffs the air and leans over to poke the woman beside me. "Wrinkly Bones One, you *are* a lazy woman, aren't you!" He turns to a boy in pre-Surge clothes, with *wings*, and squeezes his shoulder. The boy winces. "Aren't you going to defend your stupid granny, Aut-Pof—"

"I'm no granny, A'!" calls the woman. "And don't

talk to my Jack like that."

Oh no. I *do* know him. ALDON. The Conqip leader lets out a thunderous laugh and drags the boy over by his wing. "The mute is *Moojag*, not your Jack. Don't you recognise his absurd little wings? Weirdo. Like grandmother, like grandson."

Moojag? My brother—Monzi! Everything feels so familiar, but I can't string my thoughts together to make any sense of them. "Stop it," I mutter, as Aldon waltzes over. "Leave him alone."

"Stupid as your brother, I see." Aldon puts his hand in his jacket pocket and presents a small pill. Perfectly round and blue with a groove down the middle. "You just need a memory pill, don't you?"

Moojag tries to speak, but not a single word comes out of his mouth. He grabs Aldon's arm and the pill drops straight into my hand. If I eat this, maybe I'll think clearly again and remember what I'm doing here. There's something I'm supposed to do—lots of things. I pop the pill into my mouth and try swallowing, but it feels like there's a huge shell jammed in my throat. I choke, coughing it right out into the livid man's hand. He shoves it straight back into my

mouth and hands me a glass of water. I drink, but the pill still won't go down. A little more, but it just floats around the roof of my mouth. I take another gulp as the man tips up the glass. The water pours fast down my throat, and finally the pill, along with the last drop. I wipe my mouth while Aldon turns to Moojag. "To Stikleby Hall. NOW." They leave the room and the door slams closed behind them.

"You have lovely eyes," says the smiley-faced woman lying beside me. "An angel." She's too kind. "When did you come, dear? Staying with us long?"

"That's your granddaughter," says another woman in the room.

"Nema," says a third one, holding a shell. A Spondylux! In front of us, a floating holograph of a girl and boy standing beside a woman who looks a lot like the one in my bed, only younger.

It's my friends, "Izzy and Adam! And..." I look back round at the woman, with a questioning stare. "Gran?"

She smiles and nods back. "Yes! What are you doing here, Nema?" Her scaly, glistening silver hand takes mine.

I sigh. "I don't know, but you're wearing my PIE skin."

"Ah, yes. Not entirely sure why. Could it have something to do with those purple ribbons in the cupboard?"

The other two string up some violet strips. They're wearing Adam and Izzy's PIEs! "We're their grannies," says the shorter one with freckles.

"That's my smart, handsome grandson," says the taller one with short frizzy hair, pointing to the holograph of Adam.

"Sophia and Stella, dear. You remember them?" I nod, but my mind's gone blank.

"You were out for a good half hour. We just got a *whatsnapchatinstatwitface* back from the kids," says Sophia. "Apparently, you're here to save a 'Moojag' and some 'Pofs'?"

Right. But... oh no, what's happening to... "My head—" I mutter, peering at Gran..

"Rest up, dear," says Sophia, stroking my hair as I close my eyes. "It's the MP. It makes you drowsy, you see."

I really need to stay awake, though. Feels weird, having to try so hard *not* to sleep. For once, I actually can't think of a single thing.

"Remember the time we went for supplies, before

the Surge," says Gran. I shake my head. "You were only small, but I took you along with me. I wore a PIE much like this one, and you had your own little toddler-sized version. The first e-skins to receive the IF function." Another thing Dad forgot to tell us about? "Jack was sworn to secrecy, of course. For all its benefits, the IF could cause all manner of trouble. You see, it completely changes your skin."

"Like changing to yellow when we've run out of energy?" I ask. "Or when it puffs up into soft pillows, or super tough ridges to protect us?" Hey, I seem to remember *everything* about PIE!

"Not the functions that keep you healthy and safe," she says. "Something even *more* genius. It mimics environments, just like the glorious octopus, camouflaging to keep itself hidden and safe from harmful predators. And for us humans, safe from the last of the dangerous Fake Worlders!" My eyes are struggling to stay open. "Remember going into the store together? You perched on my shoulders, the pair of us completely invisible! What a team we made. Just throwing everything straight into our backpacks, not the silly SmartCart, and without scanning a single QR code…"

"Stealing, Gran?" I whisper loudly in her ear.

"Nothing of the sort! Just a little experiment. We donated everything to the shelter, of course. But you couldn't tolerate the drill of the alarms, so we didn't try that again. We drove those shopping sensors crazy," she adds with a chuckle. "I'm sure the poor robot working the cameras couldn't believe its digital eyes. By the time a human turned up, they could only watch as our bags flew magically up over Highgate River, off into the distance and out of sight."

The door clicks open and a man dressed in a striped pre-Surge suit walks in. "It's time to get those missed Gajooms."

"Isaac, my boy, is that you?" asks Stella. "I simply adore legumes, darling. Is it luncheon already?"

"It's just me, Biermont," says the man. He nods to them and walks over to me. "And that's *Gajooms*, not legumes," he adds, glancing back. "Moojag said you got the antidote strips?" Gran grins, pointing to the open wardrobe full of purple strips. "Ah, yes, very good," he says, placing his hands on our shoulders. He seems to know who I am. He's not like the other men, though. "The unwrapped Gajooms are on their way back to the factory. Moojag will meet you there in ten."

"MP, though," calls Stella, brow raised and pointing at me. "Fifteen minutes ago."

"Oh dear," says the man, inspecting my eyes and waving his hand in front of my face. "I'm Biermont, remember—the *good* Conqip?" I hear his words and want to trust them, but something feels off.

"Is it eggs?" asks Sophia, leaping out of her bed and perching on the end of ours.

"This guy wants to get sticks and strips," says Gran.

"*Does* he indeed?" exclaims Stella, crossing their arms. "Where's my Isaac disappeared to now? He promised me a *proper* lunch. He's a Big Con, you know…"

I try sitting up but my arms have gone totally limp. I shake my head. Gran leaps over me, out of bed, and declares, "We've got PIEs now. *We'll* take her." I roll over, curling up like a hedgehog, and pull the bed cover over my head. But a corner of it lifts back up and a wrinkly face zooms in, making me jump. Again. "Wakey, wakey, Sleeping Beauty."

What's that strange sound now? Like something tacky peeling away from the floor. And a sweet liquorice scent wafting in through the open door. It shoots straight up my nose before I fall straight back to sl…

10

WRINKLY WRANGLERS

The muffled voices of Gran and her friends brush my ears as I open my eyes, but all I see is the ceiling. I look to the left. Is that the top of the door? But I'm still lying down—and I'm not on the bed, or the floor! My heart sinks to my stomach. "Don't panic," says a familiar voice, as I prepare to plummet. "I've got you." It's Gran, propping up my entire body over her head with her hands! "Sophia and Stella, bring the strips! We're off to stripe some Gajooms. Whatever *that* means…" My head hangs back as Gran points to the upside-down door and flies me out of the upside-down room, like a busy pre-Surge waiter carrying a ginormous tray on one hand!

"Good luck," calls out a man behind us. "See you on the upside." The 'upside'? So this is the downside, then?

I do kind of remember going underground. But what's Gran doing here?

Animals' heads and portraits of pre-Surge businessmen fly past me through the long, dimly-lit room. Straight out of there, we make down a tunnel, and at the end come to a wall with a round panel labelled 'URAQT'... You Are A Cutie?... Oh! Giant rock candy stick robots!... The sweet factory!... We're in Gajoomdom!

"I do hope you remember how to stripe sticks, Nema," says the tall one. Yes, now I remember—Stella.

"I'm sure she'll do a wonderful job," says the kind woman... Sophia!

Gran sets me down and holds me steady by the shoulders. "She's my granddaughter. Of course she will." Gran raises her arm to draw a circle in the air. The panel slides open and a bright strawberry scented light shines through the gap as it rotates up. I peek inside. A throng of giant, bendy, purple-and-white striped Gajoomstiks bound around a conveyor belt strewn with multi-coloured sweets.

"*Bienvenue!*" calls Moojag, appearing in front of me and holding out a handful of treats. I take one of the yellow bonbons and pop it in my mouth. Lemon and lime fizzes on my tongue. He grins. "*Bonjour*, Sis." Smiling back, I take his hand and climb through the window into the factory. Our feet slurp and suction across the sticky factory floor as we pass the busy, giant candy stick workers. He stops in front of a group of white ones. "Stripe here!" he exclaims, pointing to the first. "And here," he adds, jabbing another. The stick jerks and stomps in front of him. "Gajoom soldier," he orders, marching around it, "make stripes, not war!"

The Auticode! *That's* why we're here. To reverse the Conqip's evil code on the last unwrapped Gajooms, so they don't attack our Real World—the upside! I point to the sticks. "The autidote?"

Moojag giggles. "*Oui! L'antidote*. They must to stripe, only then revert to peaceful selves."

I grab a purple liquorice strip from Sophia, while Moojag pins the Gajoom down, and wrap it round and round the 'stik as he rolls it along the ground. Gran leaps forward with Sophia to grab another one, but it slips right through their arms and does a figure of eight dance around them. Sophia tries stroking the 'stik, but it jolts back and pounds the floor, smashing the crunching candy beneath it. I glance away as Gran lunges forward and punches the 'stik to the ground. Sophia quickly jumps in and wraps it as it turns. The last three smaller Gajooms swivel round and *gajoom stik* for the door. Stella grabs one and climbs onto its back, like they're mounting a horse (you can tell its back side,

from the direction it's going in). They throw Moojag and I two strips and we leap onto the last pair, waving our Gajoom stripes in the air like lassos. Stella leaps off the 'stik, and just before it reaches the door, runs round and round it so that the stripe winds up all over it in a perfect spiral. Moojag sorts the second, and I, the last. Good work! Sure, my stripes aren't as clean as Stella's, or as cool as Moojag's wavy zig-zag design, but that should do the job.

The freshly striped mini-Gajooms jiggle and give us each a little nudge, as if to say 'thank you'. Moojag clasps his hands and nods back. "To the Switching Room," he says, turning for the door. We follow him out of the factory and into another room, smaller and hexagonal-shaped, with doors on each of its six walls.

11

MP MARSHMALLOW

"They're here, in the Switching Room," cries a shrill but timid voice. The little orange Pof, sat cross-legged in the centre, holds a smartphone right up in her face. "Real World lizards, Sir!"

Moojag zooms up to her and grabs the device before she can turn the camera on us. "Shhh, *petite* Pof. They are here to rescue you!"

"Aldon said they would come," she whispers in his ear. "Big reward for catching a Real Worlder—one HUNDRED chocolate oranges!"

"Poof Poof, Kitty, and Rania have already gone," I explain, kneeling down.

"Traitor," sniffs the Pof. She leaps up, making Moojag jump, and pirouettes round him.

"We came back for the rest of you," I add, pointing up. "There are all kinds of sweet fruit waiting for you in the Real World! Just like this..." Oh no—where's the pineapple gone? I glance at Moojag. "The pineapple!" I whisper. "We need it to get Deja."

My brother lifts his waistcoat and jiggles. "This little thing?" he asks, pulling out the spiky fruit and handing it to me with a grin. He turns back to the Pof. "Where is Deja?"

"Manning the ticket office at Stikleby," she says, showing us her video from the Conqip Awards. "Aren't they *amazing*. Brix is *so* brave. *So* handsome. *So* clever!" Is she honestly talking about Brix? I wonder what award *he* gave himself. "He won the Sexiest Conqip Award, of course." *Of course*.

"To Stikleby Hall, all," whispers Moojag.

"But the Conqip will see us." I look round at the doors and spot 'T42', the one for Pof Palace. "We should go to the palace and wait there for all the Pofs."

"I'm always welcome at the Palace, dear," declares Stella. "There every Thursday for tea with William."

"Not Nonsuch Palace," says Gran. "The Palace of the Pofs! Whoever *they* are."

Sophia smiles, waving at the little orange girl. "Adorable Mights like this one," she says. Orange Pof giggles, raising her arms to flex her muscles at us, when her phone chimes. "We should go," I say, showing everyone the door. But a dozen Pofs fly in, carrying an enormous net. They drop it down over us and pull on some strings so that it closes up tight beneath our feet. We fall and crash into each other as we're flown up, inside the swinging trap, and out of the room. Wait, this has happened before! And that time we ended up in a... Marshmallow Chamber! The memory of a damp dungeon, drowning in marshmallow gunk with the sound of Izzy's fart-filled bubbles going pop, fills my head.

My PIE has almost turned grey; Adam and Izzy's, too: they're running out of juice. Everything goes quiet as a round hatch flips open in the floor below us and we're dropped out of the net, straight into that very same chamber of thick bubbling marshmallow. But it isn't pink any more. This time, it's bright blue!

Moojag peers down at us, shaking his head. "*Mon dieu*, MP marshmallow. Do not eat, Sis. Full of blue pills, it is..." I spit out the toxic-looking goo that's crept into my mouth. But Sophia is already munching it. Hmm.

Like grandmother, like granddaughter! And now Stella and Gran are eating it too.

"Moojag!" I call back up. But my brother's gone already and the door slams shut. Gran squints through her blue goo-laced eyes and tuts at Sophia and Stella both dozing off. Their bodies start to sink, heads barely sticking out of the gunk now. "Keep your arms and legs moving. Otherwise you'll sink even lower!"

"Aren't you lovely," says Gran, licking the marshmallow off her blue lips.

"Thank you," I answer, watching her eyes focus on me as I wait for her to ask who I am.

"Do you come down here often?"

"Not if I can help it," I say, grabbing hold of her shoulder to keep her upright.

"I feel quite tired, girl. See you in the morning."

"NO—you can't sleep. You've got to stay awake!" Gran just yawns and pulls her hand out of the goo to give me a little wave, when the hatch creaks back open, filling the chamber with light.

"I hear we have a Wrinkly Bones thief, now?" calls a hoarse voice from above. An old man peers inside.

The Conqip with the fiercely receding hairline that's impossible to forget—Aldon. "They aren't really worth saving," he says, throwing down a rope. "But *you* are the one who's supposed to be down there, not them. Idiot Pofs. Now," he adds, snapping his fingers three times, "WAKE UP, Wrinkly Bones!"

Gran's eyelids fling open. "Father?" she calls. Aldon huffs. She glances at me with happy but tired red eyes. "Look," she says, gazing up, "Father has come for me."

"Take the rope, Avti!" Aldon calls down. I grab Gran's hands and help her clutch on to the rope. Her body rises up slowly out of the marshmallow as another two ropes drop down from the hatch. I haul over a drowsy Sophia and Stella and wrap their stubborn, bony fingers around the ropes. "See you soon," I whisper into Sophia's ear.

"You're a good girl, Izzy," she says, stroking my head with her gooey blue hand.

"Okay," I say. But it looks like there's no rope coming for me, so I guess not everyone agrees.

"Hardly a ten-star spa resort, *is* it," Stella whispers, smirking at Sophia, before they're both plucked from the chamber at once.

"Goodbye, naughty girl," calls Aldon, slamming the hatch door and leaving me down here, all alone.

My head feels fuzzy. Everything's starting to blur. More of the blue must have seeped into my mouth. Moojag will come for me, though, just like he did last time. He has to. If I can just stay awake a little longer... I can't fall asleep... I won't fall asleep... I mustn't fall asleep... I'm falling asl...

A TASTE OF YOUR OWN MEDICINE

"Sister!" Moojag calls, clicking his fingers right in front of my eyes. I pull myself up and stretch with a yawn, like I've slept a thousand years. It *feels* a thousand years since I felt like this. "Wakey wakey time," he says, perched on the edge of the bed. "You're no longer in the Marshmallow Chamber, Nem."

"I knew you'd come back for me."

"*Pas moi*. T'was Nem Avti," he says, pointing to Gran.

She shakes her head and grins. "T'was the Invisibility Function."

"While you were in the clouds, Sleeping Beauty," Sophia pipes up, "we hatched a plan."

"Aldon will be on his way any moment," adds Stella, before I can ask what that plan is.

"But he'll find me!"

"Good," says Gran.

"Good?"

"Yes. All part of our brilliant idea." I'm not sure I like the sound of this plan. "All you need do is pop into the corridor and call out for him and his two monkeys." Travis and Brix? Hmm, things seem to be coming back to me now. I frown at her. "Yes. Do it right away," she says, nodding and shaking her fist. "Time is of the essence." Everything's always such a rush down here. If only I could be back up in the safe and peaceful Real World. No drama. Forget saving the world. Forget saving a bunch of little winged people—who could save themselves, if only they knew they had it in them. If I could just not be here, for one solitary, single second.

Sophia takes my hand and ushers me to the door. I edge round to peer out into the hallway. It's empty. No sign of either Conqip or Pof. I open my mouth to call something, anything, but not a sound gets out. I turn back.

"You can do it!" exclaims Moojag, cupping his

12

A TASTE OF YOUR OWN MEDICINE

"Sister!" Moojag calls, clicking his fingers right in front of my eyes. I pull myself up and stretch with a yawn, like I've slept a thousand years. It *feels* a thousand years since I felt like this. "Wakey wakey time," he says, perched on the edge of the bed. "You're no longer in the Marshmallow Chamber, Nem."

"I knew you'd come back for me."

"*Pas moi*. T'was Nem Avti," he says, pointing to Gran.

She shakes her head and grins. "T'was the Invisibility Function."

"While you were in the clouds, Sleeping Beauty," Sophia pipes up, "we hatched a plan."

"Aldon will be on his way any moment," adds Stella, before I can ask what that plan is.

"But he'll find me!"

"Good," says Gran.

"Good?"

"Yes. All part of our brilliant idea." I'm not sure I like the sound of this plan. "All you need do is pop into the corridor and call out for him and his two monkeys." Travis and Brix? Hmm, things seem to be coming back to me now. I frown at her. "Yes. Do it right away," she says, nodding and shaking her fist. "Time is of the essence." Everything's always such a rush down here. If only I could be back up in the safe and peaceful Real World. No drama. Forget saving the world. Forget saving a bunch of little winged people—who could save themselves, if only they knew they had it in them. If I could just not be here, for one solitary, single second.

Sophia takes my hand and ushers me to the door. I edge round to peer out into the hallway. It's empty. No sign of either Conqip or Pof. I open my mouth to call something, anything, but not a sound gets out. I turn back.

"You can do it!" exclaims Moojag, cupping his

hands like a funnel round his mouth.

"*ALDON,*" I scream so loud, the whole of Gajoomdom can probably hear. "TRAVIS! BRIX! I'm in the Ward! Come get me!" Wait, what am I saying! I look back into the room, at everyone clapping. Outside, the thunder of half a dozen heavy feet stomping into Conqip Hall. How can this be good?

The scent of sweaty men fills the air as they pound the ground, turning the corner for the Ward—and *me*. I dash back in and jump into bed, pulling my knees up to my chest and clutching the covers up over me. I look round for Gran but she's gone. Moojag winks and climbs into the cupboard again. Sophia? *Gone*. Stella? *Gone*. How could they do this to me?

"What in the world is going on!" shouts Aldon, striding in with his cane.

Gran wouldn't leave me alone with the Conqips. I have to trust the plan, whatever it is. "Here I am," I say, as though I don't care what happens to me, while my whole body trembles.

"I don't like games, little girl," he says, stabbing the floor with his walking cane. "Where are the Wrinklies? How did you—" His top lip curls up and mouth opens wide, but it doesn't seem like he wants it to. He shakes his head and tries to speak, but his jaws stretch wide apart and one of those little blue pills appears out of nowhere, flying straight for his mouth. There is no *nowhere*, though, is there, Gran? Is that you? The *invisible* you!?

Aldon snarls at me. "Wipe that stupid grin off your face, child," he says, choking as he swallows the pill. "For heaven's sake, idiots, get me some fluids! I think I've swallowed a blasted fly."

Brix strides over to pass Aldon a silver flask. "Let's finish off the brat," he says, grinning at me, "once and for all."

"Not just yet. She could be useful when we finally invade the creepy Real World."

"I won't help," I utter. "Selfish, greedy men don't deserve to live in the Real World."

"Shut that dirty little mouth!" shouts Brix, looking back at Conqip III in the doorway.

Travis steps forward and walks directly over to me. He has darker circles under his eyes now and somehow doesn't seem as nasty as I remember. Still, he reaches

out to slap me in the face. Instead, his arm falls down, slamming into his side, and his head swings out to the right. "OUCH!" he cries, caressing his cheek with the other hand. "The witch just slapped me!"

"I didn't!"

Travis' lips stretch outward and his mouth opens wide. A pill floats inside and his lips purse together as though he's about to blow a raspberry. He shakes his head violently, trying to open his mouth.

"BRIX," yells Aldon, "shut that little tyrant up, RIGHT NOW. Before I slap the *three* of you!"

Brix sways forward, like a model walking a pre-Surge catwalk, and swings back his arm. But the arm just sticks there beside him in mid-air. He looks like a pre-Surge policeman directing traffic. Travis sniggers. I would *so* love to join him right now.

"What the devil is the matter with you, Brix?" asks Aldon.

"I seem to be stuck, A'. Something's got me!" Another little pill appears, flying directly into Brix's open mouth. He grabs at his throat, swallowing unwillingly, and glares back at Travis.

"For heaven's sake," says Aldon, sneering at them. He marches toward me, but slows as he approaches, and drops to his knees right in front of the bed. Grabbing at the rail, he lets out a string of words: "Bones... witchcraft... get back-up!..." before collapsing onto the floor.

Travis and Brix turn for the door but tumble to the ground before they even reach it, and fall fast asleep right there on the spot. I breathe a sigh of relief and leap out of bed to creep over to the cupboard and open its door.

"Is it done?" asks Moojag, peering out.

"If 'done' is three flat-out Conqips, then, yes, it's done."

He clasps his hands and looks round the room. "And *Grand-maman*?"

"Right here," calls Gran, appearing out of somewhere with Sophia.

"*Soooo* much fun," says Sophia.

"Thrills 'n' spills, men and pills," chants Moojag.

I point to the sorry heap of men. "What are you going to do with them?"

"Get them in," demands Gran, calling Moojag over. He heaves each of the bodies onto the beds and pulls the covers up and over their faces. "You," she says, squinting as though it's the first time she's ever seen me. She looks suspiciously up and down my grey nightie. "In the cupboard," she orders, opening the door, "with the winged boy!" Stella drops out, looking confused. I shrug my shoulders, climbing into the wardrobe with Moojag before Gran closes us both in and the Ward door swings open.

THREE BAD WOLVES

The door bangs against the wall and a girl wanders in, singing, "Tea for three, and three for tea!" She won't be so cheery when she finds Conqips in the Wrinklies' beds. I hope Gran and the other two are out of sight—PIE's juice will run out real soon. "*My*, what bushy eyebrows you have today, Wrinkly Bones One! Come on, wakey-wakey now... *My*, what a thin head of hair you have today, Wrinkly Bones Two! Hmm. Why are they all still sleeping? Aldon is right! They really are such *lazy* bones... *My*, what big ears you have, Wrinkly Bones Three! I suppose I'll just be leaving the tray for you here, then. I really mustn't miss Great Aldon's award..." The Pof's nattering trails off as she heads out of the room and the door slams shut again.

I push the cupboard door open to find all three grannies wandering aimlessly round the room and the three Conqip sound asleep, like big babies in their big cots. What kind of nightmare is this?

"Man in my bed!" calls Stella, whipping the cover off Travis.

"Don't wake their precious hearts," whispers Sophia, pulling it back up over him and stroking back his quiff. Their precious *what*, now?

"One in mine, too," says Gran.

"But you just put them there," I say, brow raised.

"*Oui*," agrees Moojag, "you *absolutement* did."

"And why would I put a wrinkly old man in my bed?" asks Gran.

"He's Aldon," I explain. "The Conqip who's kept you in here for years and tried twice now to drown me in marshmallow!"

Sophia whispers in her ear. Gran peers back at me. "Nema?"

"Yes."

She stares, squinting, and scans my face. "Well, why didn't you say so! My eyes aren't as good as they used to be, darling."

"That's all right, Gran," I say, leaning in for a hug. She wraps her spindly arms around me and puckers her lips before kissing my cheek. I turn to wipe away the kiss with the back of my hand.

"We gave them the MPs," says Stella, finally remembering the plan. "Now we simply have to wait."

"For what?" I ask.

"A little taste of their own medicine." Hmm. I'm pretty sure they got that already.

"If we're to get out of here," explains Sophia, "we must trick them."

"If you want the Conqip to leave you alone," adds Gran, tapping the side of her head, "all you've to do is target their weak spot."

A drowsy Brix in Sophia's bed rouses. "My mimosa," he calls from beneath the covers, "at once!"

"Your champagne breakfast will be along shortly, sir," Stella calls back with a wink from their bed. "The service is rather poor, though. It has to be said."

Brix shakes his head, trying to get up, but Sophia is holding him down firmly by the wrists. "What's the meaning of this, old lady," he says, veins bulging from his neck. "And why the hell are you wearing trashy Real World skins?"

"Calm now," says Sophia, "or you'll have yourself an aneurysm!"

"I'm *quite* calm, thank you," he says, head falling straight back down to hit the pillow. Sophia pulls a small bottle from under the mattress and takes out a pill. She pops it in his mouth and turns to Travis now stirring in Stella's bed.

"Here you go, dear," says Stella, popping an MP into his mouth, too. "Not quite caviar, but it'll make you feel just as queasy." He gazes up at them, wobbles his head and falls back to sleep.

Now Aldon's groaning again. We all wander over and sit in a row along the edge of his bed. "Good morning," says Gran, perched right beside his head. "Remember me?"

"Mother?" he asks, peering up at her.

Moojag turns to me and whispers loudly, "Triple dose." I lift my hand to brush away the sound and cover my ear.

"Yes, dear. I am Deirdre, your mother. You've been a very naughty boy, haven't you?" That's weird. Why would

she call his mother 'Deirdre'? *Her* mum's name. My great grandmother. Has she forgotten who he is again?

"I didn't do it, Mother," he whispers, pointing to Brix. "It's *him*."

"It isn't kind to blame other people," says Sophia.

"Why don't you get out of bed and go play," suggests Gran.

Aldon tries to get up, but he can't move. He can barely even lift his head. "DON'T BE SO LAZY!" shouts Stella.

"I'm not," whimpers poor Aldon, "I can't!" I know I shouldn't feel sorry for the man, but he looks so weak now. Not at all the nasty piece of work he was before. He turns and lifts his arm to guard his face.

"You ought to be ashamed," says Gran, pulling his bed cover back down. "Letting yourself go like this." She points to his middle. "Just look at that." What exactly are we looking at?

"I know," laughs Stella, "and the hair. Well, what's left of it!" True, there isn't much of that.

"He looks like a shrimp," adds Sophia, giggling. Hmm. How does he look like a shrimp?

"Perhaps not a shrimp," says Gran. "More like a gigantic blubber whale." Aldon's long face drops even lower and he begins to cry. Does he really deserve this? Poor blubber whale, though, being compared to Aldon!

"He'll pay for what he's done," says Stella. "What goes around comes around, kid." Wow. It's hard telling who's Conqip and who's not now!

"I haven't done *anything*, I promise," he says.

"Well, quite," says Gran. "And you won't," she adds, crossing her arms. "In fact, you're going to achieve nothing special whatsoever in your life. You're not only lazy; you're rude, selfish, greedy, not to mention hideous, and much, *much*, too tall." Okay, now that's going too far.

We step away from the bed as Aldon leans over, retching. His face has turned a corpse-like pale. Moojag pulls a handkerchief from his waistcoat pocket and passes it to Gran. She wipes the vomit dribbling off Aldon's chin and shoves him back up onto the bed.

I don't remember Gran ever being quite so cruel. She doesn't mean any of it, I'm sure. She's a very good actor, though. They all are.

"I'm sure he's sorry," I say.

"I'm sure he's *not*," says Stella, crossing their arms. "He'll stay here until he's learned his lesson and is ready to do some *honest* work."

Aldon gazes at Gran. She nods as he lowers his eyes. "I'll be good, I promise," he says, sobbing. "Don't mean to be rude. Ever so sorry, Mother." He makes a lot of promises, doesn't he! I wonder how many promises he's actually kept in his entire life.

"So you should be…" says Gran, popping yet another pill in his mouth, "sorry. Now, get some rest, and if you're a very good boy, we'll be back soon with another treat for you."

Aldon swallows, rolls over, and pulls the covers up over his head. I'm not sure any kind of treat would make much difference to how he's feeling right now, though. Especially not a blue one! Will he even remember any of this when the pills wear off? If they *ever* do.

"Time to go," says Gran. I nod and turn for the door with Moojag, but she doesn't move. None of them do.

"Come on, then," I call back.

"We can't," says Sophia, wide-eyed, crouched on the floor. The PIEs have turned grey. They can't get up.

"You'll have to go without us," says Gran, raising a frail arm.

"No, wait," I say, stepping back. "The Pofs said you *can* walk. Your bodies have just forgotten how."

"You go," says Stella. "My Isaac will be along shortly, to take us all out for that cream tea at the Ritz. He promised."

They've remembered they can't walk, and that's probably made them lose their sense of time again, too. I look round at Moojag standing in his yogic tree pose, and cock my head. "Stretching," he says, sticking out his leg and holding it there. He lowers it back down, then takes Gran's foot, straightens out her leg and gently raises it up and down five times. She lifts her other leg on her own. I nod encouragingly as I watch her slowly lift it up and down, all by herself, over and over, while Moojag gets to work on the other grannies.

"But they'd need weeks of stretching," I say, "before they could walk even just a few steps. Wouldn't they?"

My brother turns to me with a wink. "Yes, they would!" he says, releasing Stella's leg and throwing up a fist. "And they have!"

14

REAL ALDON

The Wrinklies smile, sticking their legs in the air and laughing at their natural power. Those exercises Pari has secretly been doing must have given them back some of the strength they lost. How great it must feel, suddenly being able to move again? Maybe it's like when you take your first ever steps. How awful, though, to suddenly remember you can't walk any more. And to have to relive the fact you can't every time you try getting up.

I link arms with Gran to walk her over to the door and then back to Aldon snivelling and repeatedly apologising. "If you weren't so lazy," she tells him, "you could walk like me."

I wonder how much he's liking the taste of his

own medicine now? What would I say, if I wanted to upset him? 'You can't stand spending time on your own'? "And no one can stand spending time with you," I say out loud, without meaning to! I step back, wide-eyed at myself, and wait for something cruel to erupt from the man.

"You're right. I'm good for nothing," he says, shaking his head. Wow. Not what I was expecting. And isn't that exactly what he called the bullied Auts?

"If you do what we say," says Gran, "you'll get all the sweets in the world."

Aldon grimaces. "Thank you, but I don't want any more sweets," he says. "They just make me feel worse."

"If you help us," Gran assures him, "everything will get back to normal again."

"I'm useless," he says.

"But not for long," she replies. "Your boys will stay here, but you'll come with us." She removes his covers and helps him sit up as Sophia feeds more pills to the other Conqips. "You can't walk, so I'll have to carry you." But you can barely walk, yourself, Gran, let alone carry a fully-grown man! I glare at her but she just turns to Moojag. "Monzi, if you would be so kind." She points to her foot and whispers,

"Back me up!" He squeezes her toe and it turns purple. Gran nods to Stella and Sophia who squeeze each other's toes. Theirs turn red and blue and the PIEs power back on. I look back at Gran and my e-skin is already sparkling silver again!

"Emergency Back-Up Drive," she says, looking very pleased with herself. "Don't tell me Jack kept that from you, too?" I nod. Why would Dad keep this from us, though? "That boy never listened to anything I told him. I bet he never even figured it out. You see, I designed PIE to organise the boring information so that we can focus on the important stuff. That way, there's always a bunch of free space for emergencies."

"Like Spoons?" I ask. Dad said that before PIE, they'd had to measure their energy levels themselves. Some people measured it in 'Spoons'. The fewer Spoons they had, out of a total of, say, ten, the less energy there was to do everyday pre-Surge work.

"Exactly," answers Gran. "Always keep spare Spoons!" Right now, I feel like I have about one and a half Spoons remaining.

Stella and Sophia call "Real World" into their Spondylux shells and hundreds of images project out in front

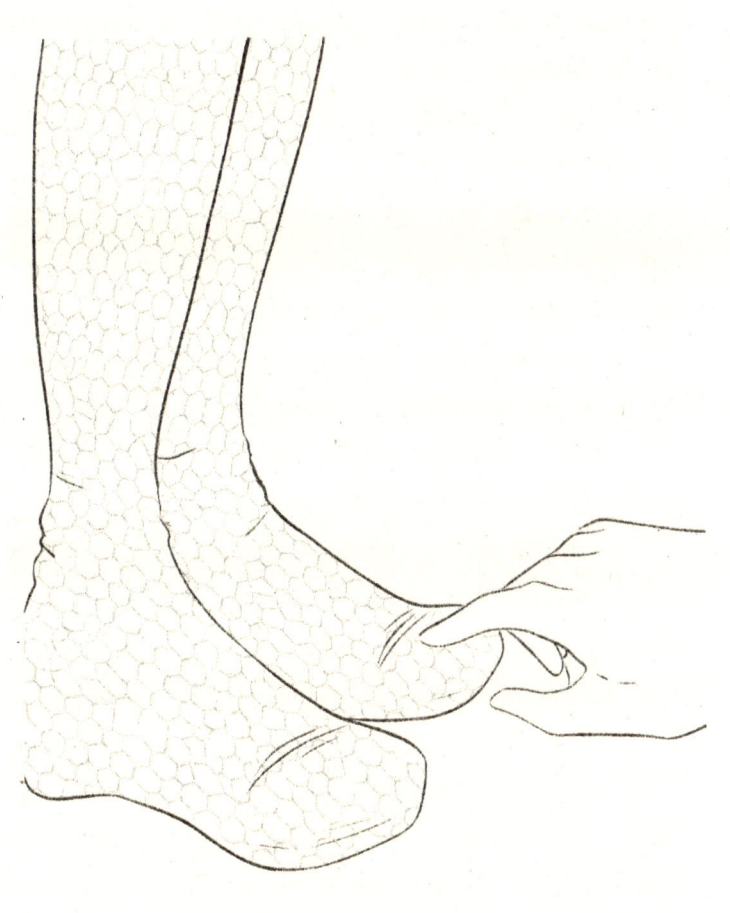

of Aldon. He shakes his head. "Why did you have to create that waste of space world up there?" Now *that* sounds more like the Aldon we know.

"Why didn't you tell me what the Conqip were up to down here?" replies Gran. "And taking the children. Monzi, too!" He shakes his head. "Brainwashing those depressed parents and kidnapping the poor kids for your own gain." Wait—why should Aldon have told *her*?

Sophia struts over and rests a hand on his shoulder. "It's never too late to change, naughty boy."

He shakes his head. "I'm bad to the bone. I'll never change." Okay, we've lost him again.

"Come on," says Stella, "It's time for you to claim your award. Don't you agree?" I wince, clamping my arms down by my sides, as they grab him right in the armpits. They lift him up and swing him over their shoulders, as though he's only a scarf. He doesn't budge, or even complain.

"I don't deserve an award," he blubbers.

"Of course you do," says Gran. "How about 'Greatest Loser of the Decade'? There must be a loser, it's only fair." What's he lost? Apart from his memory, of course.

"That's life," agrees Sophia.

"But that's not fair," I say.

"Life *isn't* fair," answers Gran. But life in RW is *always* fair! My head feels a sticky mess, like a big ball of knotted candyfloss. The sooner we get out of here, the better. "Aldon, you look confused," says Gran. "Do you understand what was said to you?"

"I heard," answers his hanging, upside-down head. "Very well, I'll accept the stupid award."

"Stupid award for a stu—"

"Yes, yes, all right."

Moojag holds the door open and Stella sprints out sideways with Aldon draped across their shoulders, closely followed by Gran and Sophia. "Home soon, Sis," my brother declares with a wink. He'd better be right. I nod, wandering out after him, and peek back in to check on the Conqips. They're fast asleep. I lock the door and pass the key to Moojag. He slips it in his waistcoat pocket and grabs my arm, before whisking me off down the corridor and out through the double doors of Conqip Hall, after the Wrinklies.

THE AWARD

Moojag whizzes us over the candy path to Stikleby Hall, where the Wrinkly Bones are propping up Aldon in front of the doors.

"Hurry up, you two," calls Gran. "He's a slippery one!" He *is* that.

Stella knocks on the door and Orange Pof instantly sticks her head out.

"We have Aldon here for his award, dear," announces Gran.

"Delicious, just in time," answers the Pof. "I adore your costume. It's *soooooo*—"

"Thank you, it's PIE."

"I *love* pie!" she exclaims, pulling the thick wooden

doors wide open. She eagerly waves everyone inside, but whizzes right into me as I step forward. "Hey, *you're* not allowed in here, weird Real World girl."

Moojag pinches her wing and spins her round. "She's my sister, piffety-pof!"

"Fine," she resigns, "but has she got sweets?"

"I haven't," I answer. Pof's brow raises and she holds up the palm of her little hand as close to my face as she possibly can. "I know where to find some, though."

She grins, saying, "See you later then, friend!" and finally lets me pass. I nod and catch up to the others with her hovering right behind. "This way!" she says, zooming up front and guiding us all along the corridor to the doors of the theatre. Two older Pofs guarding the entrance whisper to each other when they see Aldon, and immediately pull the doors open.

Orange Pof flies down the aisle, between packed rows of buzzing Pofs eating multi-coloured popcorn, and swerves up onto the stage. "Our great and wonderful Aldon has arrived!" Everyone cheers as the grannies haul him up and over to the podium.

A Pof slips in through the curtains. She's yellow

from head to foot. Yellow trilby hat covered in yellow feathers. Yellow eyeshadow and lipstick. A yellow animal-print cashmere polo neck, all fluffy like a newborn chick. Her tutu is, yes, yellow, with almond-shaped pleats that flap as she skips, like the petals of a flower swaying in the breeze. Yellow tights dressed with yellow-and-white striped leg warmers, finished with mellow yellow pumps. "And, finally," the girl announces with a twirl, "time to announce the winner of our most coveted award... The Aldon." She unclips the clasp of her yellow handbag, hanging by a strap across her body, and pulls out a large gold envelope. She opens it and reads, "The winner of this year's Aldon—The Greatest Leader Award—is... ALDON!" She laughs like a hyena and hovers haphazardly around him.

Aldon leans awkwardly against the podium. He can barely stand up straight and his head is flopped over his shoulder. "Thank you Pofs, Gajooms, and fellow Conqip. But I can not accept the award this time." A humongous wave of shock vibrates through the theatre. Pofs gossip among themselves; Gajooms bow their heads (or are they bottoms?); Conqips whisper to each other, looking suspiciously about the room.

"Is everything all right, Aldon?" one of them calls from the front row. The man steps into the aisle. "Not the usual way of things, sir..." Their fellow Conqips nod in agreement.

"Yes, yes, everything's quite all right."

Gran leaps to the stage, glowing in my PIE. "Aldon has decided to dedicate his award to someone more deserving this year." She glances at him, brows raised. He returns a pathetic nod and beckons Yellow Pof. "Your name, winged girl?"

"Deja," she replies, nodding her dizzy head. She hovers over to Gran and whispers, "Are you all right, Wrinkly Bones One? Why aren't you all in bed sleeping, like good girls?" She eyes us beside the stage below them.

"Dear Deja," answers Gran, gazing out into the audience. "We are cured! We can walk; *run*, even!" She sprints to the end of the stage and back again. "You see?" she calls out, pointing down at WB2 and WB3 before turning to me. "This dear Real Worlder, our very own Zoe, brought us some *magic* clothes."

The Pofs whizz up from their seats and hover round the grannies to inspect the skins. "This one belongs to that

Real Worlder, Nema," says a Pof boy with small wings, poking Gran. She looks over at me, then looks away, trying to remember. She smiles and looks back with a nod.

Deja checks out Wrinkly Bones Two and Three and a whiff of juicy pineapple wafts over us as she waves her yellow-gloved hands and sticks them on her hips. "And the others are wearing her friends' clothes!" she cries, glaring back at Aldon. "The one who tried to take us to the Real World!" The man can barely stay upright now, one arm hooked around Gran's shoulders. Deja's cicada biceps bulge through her yellow sleeves as she grips his other arm and hauls him up so that his feet barely touch the ground.

"What is important, now, dear Pofs, Gajooms, and Conqip," continues Gran, "is that Aldon is kindly giving away his award."

Silence. The Conqip look to each other in disbelief. One whispers "Where's Brix?" to their Conqip neighbour. The other shakes his head. "And Travis!" They look behind them and over at us. How can any of this be a good idea! I shuffle between Stella and Sophia and peer up at Gran, who's prodding Aldon.

"So, Aldon," says Gran, "who is your award going

to this year?" She cocks her head in my direction and prods him again. "Remember what you told us," she says. "You're not worthy. You're lazy, greedy; nobody cares about you any more. Isn't that right, A'?" The lines of his forehead scrunch up as he conjures a pained smile. She nods. He looks really tired now and his skin has literally turned the colour of snot. Gran prods him again and points down at me. She almost looks pleased with herself. But I feel quite sick.

"The award," Aldon says, head hanging down and looking right at me, "goes to… Nema." Subtle, Gran. I peer round, without turning my head. Every single pair of eyes in the room have zoomed in on *me*. Brows raised. Mouths ajar. A cloud of Pofs buzz overhead, none of them cheering. Do I really have to go up there? In front of everyone? And say what? I look down at the nightie I'm still wearing and my wonky toes. Gran waves me up. Stella and Sophia grab my hands, drag me on to the stage and pull up my arms. This is just ridiculous. It's not like I've done anything.

I can't see for Pofs whizzing all about. I can't hear for Gajooms stomping the floor. I shudder at the confused pineapple and liquorice scented fumes filling my nostrils.

A Conqip leaps up from his seat in the front row, followed by all the others. "They've got Brix and Travis!" he shouts. Aldon waves a weak arm and shakes his head, but they take no notice. It's as though, suddenly, he's not their leader any more. But it definitely isn't *me*, either. They must have realised he's not himself. Well, not the Aldon *they* know, anyway.

Orange Pof zooms over to them. "If I got another chocolate orange," she says giggling, "I *might* tell you where Conqip II and III are!"

The Conqip beside her digs around inside his jacket pocket and pulls out a fistful of bonbons. He spreads the sweets across the palm of his hand and picks out the orange one. "Tell us *now*, and when we find them, you'll have all the chocolate orange you want." Why do I get the feeling she'll never get a single one?

Orange Pof curtseys and nabs the sweet from him, before hovering off down the aisle followed by a dozen Conqip. Meanwhile, another six men march onto the stage, ferrying Aldon off to the side and fencing their way round us.

16

PINEAPPLE DROPS

"Guard the traitors," a Conqip orders the Pofs, "until we decide what to do with them." Deja ruffles her wings and bows. She beckons some of her Pof friends to surround us before the Conqips march off.

I shuffle up to Gran. "What now, Nem Avti?"

She just grins back at me and winks at Sophia, who winks at Stella, who holds up a little white bottle in the air and shakes it hard.

Gran nods. "Who wants a pineapple drop?" Those aren't candy drops, though, are they, Gran! She presses a finger to her pursed lips and shakes her head at me as Stella flicks the lid open and showers the stage with pills. The Pofs zoom in scrambling for the 'sweets' and gobble them up.

How will we get them out of Gajoomdom, now, if they're all asleep—or, worse, in a coma! I look for Gran. She's wandered off to the other side of the stage to talk to Aldon. I leave Moojag and Stella lining up the Pofs' dizzy bodies into two neat rows, and join Gran with Sophia.

"Your Conqip friends too mean to take you with them?" Gran teases Aldon.

Hunched over and head hanging down, he peers up at her, and then over at me and Sophia. "It won't last," he says, "your perfect world. Nothing ever does."

"Bundle of fun, isn't he," says Gran, handing him another blue pill. "And how's *your* little project going?"

He takes the pill and swallows it. "Take me home, Avti, back to London Tops. I'm tired. Let someone else deal with this candy disaster."

"Sorry," says Sophia, "but you're not getting off *that* easy."

Is she sorry, though? How come Gran isn't more angry with him, and why on earth is he doing everything she says? Nothing makes sense. It can't be the pills. They only make you sleep and forget stuff. Like where you live and who you are.

"Time to get out of here," says Gran, "before Brix and Travis come round."

"We're not leaving without the Pofs, this time," I say, crossing my arms. Moojag whizzes over and hands me the key for the Ward. "Better hurry then, Sis," he says, brows raised. "Pineapple. Ward. Ward…robe!"

Pineapple. Ward. Ward…robe? What *is* he on about? He unbuttons and opens his waistcoat. No pineapple. "You mean it's in the Ward?"

Moojag looks away and whispers, "Ward robe."

"Wardrobe?" He nods. "We have to go back to the Ward," I say, turning to Gran.

"Are you out of your mind, dear! Whatever for?"

"It's the only way to get the Pofs to come," I explain. "Poof Poof said 'Deja will do anything for a real pineapple'."

"'And where Deja goes'," continues Moojag, "'the others follow'!" I nod to him and smile.

"We have some time, anyway, before the Pofs come round."

Gran looks down at Aldon crouched on the floor beside her. "Okay. You and me," she says, nudging Moojag, "Let's go. With IF and *whatsnapchatinstatwitface* we can all stay connected." Aldon rolls his eyes and looks away.

Sophia gives her a thumbs-up. "Good. Nema and Aldon will stay with us while we watch over those darling Pofs."

"If the Conqips return," says Gran, "you know what to do."

"Be careful," I warn her. "Just grab the pineapple and come straight back, okay?"

Moojag salutes us and Gran nods. "Of course," she says. "You'll see us in a minute!" We won't, though, Gran, will we! Not in a *minute*.

Sophia bends down to lift giant baby Aldon up into her arms and we wander over to the Pofs as Gran and Moojag bolt out of the theatre.

Stella calls *"whatsnapchatinstatwitface,"* into their Spondylux. Wait, PIE streams video in emergency mode, too!? I stare, wide-eyed at the grannies nodding and a moving image of the Conqips' dining room projecting out in front of us.

Moojag spins in front of Gran's Spondylux cam to wave at us. "Now you see me..." he calls, before disappearing, "now, you don't!"

"*Shush*," whispers Gran.

"Where are you?" I ask.

"Right here." But I only see a key floating in mid air... Oh! The Invisibility Function.

"What?" asks Moojag.

"Never mind," whispers the key, "just try to act normal."

"I cannot promise that. I am Moojag!"

DEJA'S PINEAPPLE

"What's that awful noise?" asks Sophia, at the sound of bellowing men's voices streaming through the *whatsnapchatinstatwitface*.

"Imbeciles," mutters Aldon, shaking his head at the quarreling Conqips. "Turns out money *can't* buy you brains."

I squeeze my eyes shut as Moojag turns the corner for the Ward—and the men.

"Have *you* got the key, boy?" one of them yells.

"*Non*. Not Moojag," my brother answers. I shake my head and peek back at the holograph. He's shooing them all away from the door now. "But I know who has!" he says, pointing at the ghostly key hovering toward them. They leap away from the door, faces pale as a sheet of pre-Surge paper.

"What the—"

"Stop fooling about, Aut!"

"How are you doing that, weirdo?"

A Conqip grabs Moojag and locks him in his arms, but bolts back when the key goes straight for them and jabs him in the neck. Moojag slips free and the key spins round to dive down into the keyhole. It turns and the door swings wide open. Moojag makes after the key for the wardrobe, past Brix and Travis, both drowsy in the grannies' beds. The wardrobe opens and dozens of nighties fling out past him. But no pineapple. The last Conqip, still standing open-mouthed and wide-eyed in the doorway, shakes his head and sprints off down the corridor after the others.

"Where is it, Jack?"

Moojag shrugs his shoulders. "I do not know," he says, pointing to the door as Gran's invisibility fades and she swings round to see who's there, "but the sprite might."

Pari Pof hovers in, cradling her face in her hands. "Mummy took it," she whispers loudly.

"Has Mummy eaten it?" asks Gran.

Pari shakes her head and turns to Moojag. "What *is* it?"

"A pineapple," he answers.

"Pineapple *what*?" she asks, scrunching up her face.

"It's an actual real pineapple," he explains. "Where the original pineapple flavour comes from."

"Does Mummy know?" she asks, gawking at him and clinging to Gran.

"I doubt it," he says. "But we need it back, otherwise you may never see another one ever again."

"Where is she?" asks Gran.

"At the awards," says Pari. "She's the boss, since Poof Poof left us for the Real World!"

Moojag nods. "Deja is going up next."

"*Nooooo…*" cries the panicked Pof, shaking her head of golden ringlets. "She can't!"

"Of course," he whispers. "All of you are going with Deja back to the Real World." He takes her tiny hand in his and pulls her out the door with him after Gran.

"Knickerbocker Glory, this way," calls Brix, smacking his lips. "Top dessert, before we all go *poof…*"

"Spotted Dick, though!" says Travis, with a groggy yawn. Why do they keep saying *poof*? What does Brix mean, we're all going to go *poof*!?

"Will you come with us, too, Moojag," mutters the Pof, "up to the Real World?"

"I need to find someone first," my brother answers, gazing back at us through Gran's Spondylux. I step back from the zoomed-in face filling the entire holograph. "*Retrouvé le* pineapple, Sis. Something *très important* I must to do."

"Moojag thinks Mum is still alive," I explain as the holograph fizzles out. "He thinks she's here in Gajoomdom."

"We have to find Wendy," says Sophia.

"Yes, right," adds Stella, scanning the Pof-covered stage floor. Didn't they hear me? "Let's see. She must be here, among the fallen Pofs."

"What does the Might look like, dear?" asks Sophia. Maybe they think it's as impossible as I do, Mum being here, and that's why they're ignoring me.

"Wendy was wearing a red leotard," I say, "when Adam, Izzy, and I met her at Pof Palace."

"I think I've found her," calls Stella, searching an all-red Pof. Wendy chuckles in her sleep as Stella pulls out a tired-looking pineapple from the Pof's skirt pouch. "It's a Vivienne," they say, pouting.

"A what?" I ask.

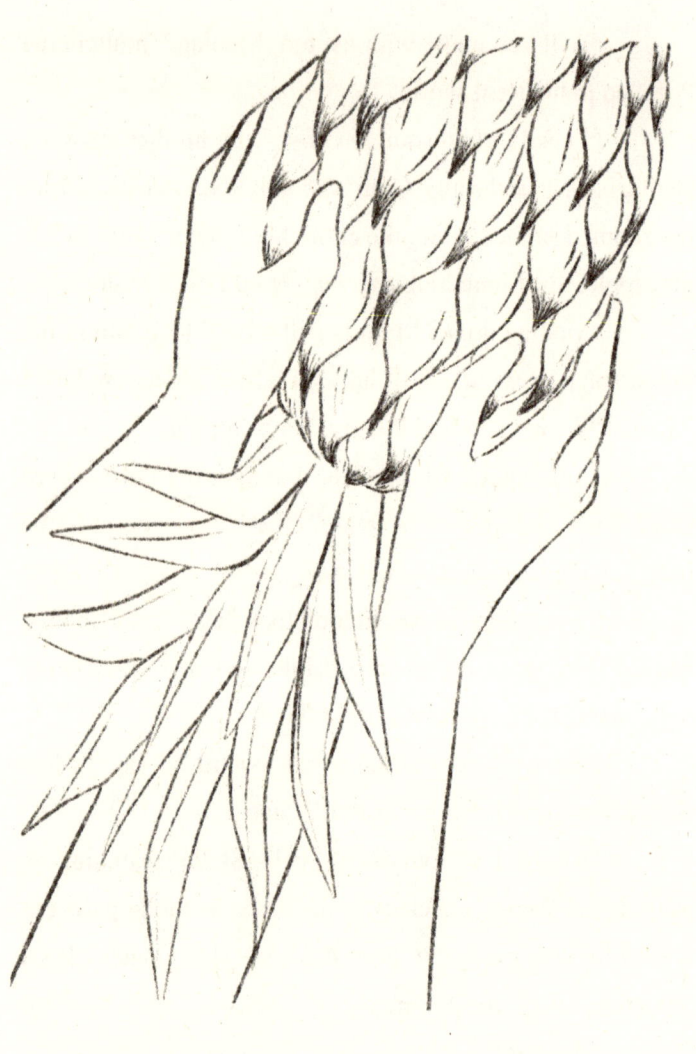

"The tutu. It's a limited edition Vivienne Westwood, darling." Stella tuts at my furrowed brow. "Iconic punk fashion designer? Dear Vivienne. Passed peacefully at home in Clapham, many years before it became Clapham Down."

"And here's Deja," says Sophia, sniffing the all-yellow Pof's hat and giggling.

I shake my head and whisper, "Don't wake her. It'll be hard keeping her from the pineapple once she sees it."

"What in the devil are you planning to do with that ugly fruit?" mutters Aldon. Stella gathers some blue pills left lying behind the podium and hands him one. He takes it and swallows. Wait—Stella's not holding the pineapple any more. I look back. Neither is Sophia. It's vanished. And so has Deja!

THE ZIZANTH
AND A TASTE OF ALDON'S OWN PIE

"Where's the pineapple?" I ask Stella.

"Deja was so quick," explains Sophia, flapping her arms in the air like wings. "She just snatched it from the podium and vanished!"

A weary Wendy bolts up and points to the rippling stage curtain. "Deja went that way," she utters.

Sophia sprints across the stage and pushes through the heavy red curtains. "Look after these," says Stella, handing me the last blue pills before chasing after her.

"Okay," I call, glancing back at Aldon who's half asleep. I check on the rest of the Pofs. They're still quiet. I sit down cross-legged on the stage between them all and wait.

"Nem Avti," mutters Aldon. "What are you playing

at, woman? How could you betray the Conqip? And *me*, your own brother!" he mumbles. "After everything we did for you. And that cosy little job with Zizanth, too, so you could fix that weird grandson of yours." The man can't know what he's saying. "You should have left the boy with his crazy mother."

I shuffle across the stage and over to his side. "He isn't weird, and she wasn't crazy," I say, guessing *weird* and *crazy* must be very mean words. And it sounds like he really *means* them, too.

"The woman still insists the geek is a genius."

"He created your Gajooms, didn't he?" I say.

"Monzi?" He laughs. "Are you out of your tiny little mind? All the autistic brat did was write some stupid code. And everything was running perfectly well down here, Avti, 'til *you* barged in. Messing with all the Pofs' heads to steal all our candy!"

Gran would never risk the Real World for sugar! "I don't even *like* candy," I say, crossing my arms.

Aldon laughs in my face and tuts. "Says the biggest hypocrite of all. Creating a world free of processed food and artificial sugar, then coming down here and stuffing yourself with sugar 'til you're blue in the face?"

I can't believe my red hot ears. It can't be true, *any* of it!

"Why are you letting me go, then?" I mutter. My heart is racing so fast, I can barely make out the words flying around inside my head.

"Because I don't have the energy any more, Avti. The other Conqips are a bunch of losers, and Deidre would never have forgiven me if I left you in that room to die."

"Your mother?"

"*Yes*, Mother!"

"And Sophia and Stella?"

"What about them? The Wrinklies brought it upon themselves, didn't they? Chasing after you like sheep."

"We found the little Might," calls Sophia, with Stella swinging Deja back in by the arms.

The bright yellow Pof ruffles her wings as they set her down, and throws up her arms. "*What.*"

"Found your gift, then," I say, pointing to the pineapple in Stella's hands. "You know what it is, right?"

"It looks weird," she answers. "But it smells of pineapple!" she adds, grinning.

"It *is* a pineapple," I say, getting back up.

"A pineapple *what*?"

"Just pineapple. The actual fruit."

Deja glares round at the grannies. They nod. "Can I try it? *Pleeeeeeease…*"

"It's all yours, if you'll just do a little something for us."

"Hypocrite," mutters Aldon. "Bribery is cheap when you're desperate, isn't it!"

What's *bribery*? Something bad, for sure. But we're helping Pofs, and that can't be wrong. I turn back to Deja. "All you have to do is come back with us to the Real World, and I promise you can have all the pineapples you can eat! For as long as they keep growing, of course."

Aldon grunts as the Pof hovers up and clasps her hands. "For reals?" she asks, gazing back down at me. "That's *all* I have to do?" I nod. She zooms over to Aldon and pokes his shoulder. "Is this a trick, Boss?"

"If Nem Avti has anything to do with it," says Aldon, brow raised.

She looks back at me. I shake my head. "It was Poof Poof's idea."

Aldon growls. "That scheming Pof witch was bound to betray us one day," he says. I pass him another pill and he accepts it with a groan. "Mother is currently turning in her grave, you know."

"Mother is just fine," calls Gran, sprinting up onto the stage.

"Mother!" he says with a jolt. "I've been a good boy, *honest*." I wonder if that man's ever spoken a true word in his entire life. "Please can we go home now?"

"Of course, dear," answers Gran. "I just have a couple more things to sort, then we can all get far, far away from this dreadful place." She sits down on the floor and peels off the silver PIE. "Put it on him," she orders me.

What? Aldon in my skin? I shake my head. "Why?"

"No time for questions, Nema. Now, help me out of it."

I suppose if she knows who I am, right now, then she probably has a good idea what she's doing. I pull the PIE down off her legs and remove Aldon's tight patent black shoes. He shakes his head as I slip it onto his feet and up just past his ankles. "Do I have to, Nem Avti?" I nod back along with Gran. He pulls it over his trousers and leans forward as

I remove his jacket to pull the skin up over his body.

"Hood, too," says Gran. He pulls it over his head and curls back up on the ground, cradling himself. "Motion off. Sound off," Gran orders Spondylux. "Moojag, dear?" she calls out. "Get up here."

My brother leaps onto the stage, out of somewhere. "*Oui?*"

"Tickle him." He looks at her, wide-eyed, and shakes his head. "It's okay, go on. Do it."

Moojag tiptoes up to the pathetic pile of Aldon and wiggles his fingers in the man's armpit. Aldon doesn't move, not even a twitch. "Not ticklish," says my astonished brother.

"*Very* ticklish!" exclaims Gran. "He just can't move. Or speak."

Moojag crawls up super close to Aldon's face. "Say something, or I tickle you again!" Aldon's pupils grow so wide that his eyes turn almost completely black.

"Now look who's 'mute'!" says Gran, crossing her arms and turning to me. "So. Do we have this pineapple?" I nod and Stella holds it up with both hands like a prize. "Good," says Gran, poking them. "Give it to Nema. You are needed in the Ward."

Stella glances at Sophia and back at Gran, scrunching up their forehead and nose.

"You'd better go with them," Gran orders Sophia. "And when you get there, *whatsnapchatinstatwitface* us."

THE TOXIC HALF

Gran leans back against the wall and sighs. She couldn't have been in on the Zizanth trials. Did she lie about everything? Was she a Conqip before? Has she known what happened to Monzi all along?

"Do you remember stuff?" I whisper to Moojag, "I mean, every detail?"

"Not the boring things," he answers. "I wish I could forget all the rest, but my mind doesn't like to let go, you know." I nod. "Like the things the Conqips say and do, and all the things I can't; the smells, the sounds; places, too." I nod.

"I don't remember much about the pre-Surge world, before losing Mum and leaving London Tops. But I'll never forget looking up at that big rainbow sign for Surrey Isles on Hampstead Harbour, the day we left. Gran promised me we'd all be together again one day, like she knew something I didn't. I believed every word." We look over at Gran. "Sometimes I even get a whiff of Captain Phil's musty sea jacket, too." Will I remember this moment, right now? Back here, underground with Moojag, Gran, and a spookily calm Aldon?

"Did you smell *her*?" asks my brother.

"Who?"

"Mum," he says, grinning. "In the Ward. Honeysuckle."

I shake my head. "I told you. None of that stuff's real. It's just your sensory memories tricking you." Funny, though: my favourite scent is honeysuckle. Is that what Mum smelled like?

Moojag huffs, traipsing over to Nem Avti and poking her. But she just points at Aldon vibrating as the whole stage lights up and Spondylux projects a *whatsnapchatinstatwitface*. It's Stella and Sophia in the Ward.

"Well, well," says Stella, spinning round. "There's

my boy, Isaac!"

Brix grunts, shoving them back. "Why are you wearing that awful PIE rubbish? You look ridiculous."

"Don't talk to your mother like that, Isaac," says Sophia, frowning at him.

He squints at her and grunts. "I'm no kid, Wrinkly Bones," he says, wafting her away. "I'm forty-five years old, woman."

"So you finally decided to show your face," says Stella.

"Don't be an idiot, Mummy," he says, tutting, "I've been here all the time. And quit with the 'Isaac'. My name is *BRIX* now."

"Brix?" asks Stella. "What ever possessed you to name yourself after a clay building block?"

"Makes perfect sense to me," says Sophia, as Moojag, Gran, and I all glance at each other, nodding. Aldon shakes his head in his hands, whilst Deja hovers round me buzzing like a cicada, hands clasped and eyes permanently fixed on the pineapple.

"Isaac is a perfectly fine name," says Stella, arms crossed. "But if Brix is what you want to call yourself,

then obviously I accept your choice. But, please," they say, extending an arm to him, "stop with all the games and just tell us what you're playing at."

"Why couldn't you ever just stay out of my business!"

"Because, my darling, however old you get, you'll always be my baby Brix." Baby Brix sounds so good, but also *so* wrong. *Baby Brix, Baby Brix, Baby Brix.*

"Get lost, Stella. I don't need this, I've very important plans to take care of."

"Such as?" asks Stella, cocking their head.

"Such as getting the hell out of this dump, and as far away from *you* as possible."

"How will you be doing that, Baby Brix?" mutters Sophia, pouting. "Your Gajoom army hasn't worked out so well, has it, dear?"

"That wasn't *my* dumb idea," he says glaring into the Spondylux. "I must be the only one with a brain in this entire kingdom. Rock candy robots, invading? Preposterous." Brix grabs Stella's wrist and pulls them over to the door. "Turn that blasted thing off," he says, covering the glowing Spondylux shell with his hand.

The hologram fizzles out and Gran leans over to release Aldon from his PIE freeze. "What's your guy Brix up to?" she asks him, squinting, as he pushes himself up against the wall. "Where's he going?"

"No idea. Whatever it is, though, it's surely much bigger than a Gajoom army." Have the blue pills worn off already?

"But Brix can't be Stella's son," I cry, "because that would mean he's Adam's dad, and Adam said he died!"

"He left when Adam was a baby," explains Gran. "But as you can see, he's still very much alive."

"Like Mum. But Mum *is* dead. *Isn't* she?"

"*Non*," Moojag fans a finger in front of my face.

"Best forget your mother," says Aldon. "The woman has a screw loose." Moojag peers round at me, glaring. It feels like there's a fireball in my chest, growing bigger and bigger, and I want to scream back, for the both of us; punch that man right in the face. But I'm zoning out. "My *sister*," says Aldon, raising a brow at Gran, "thinks Zoe is God's gift."

Sister!? No. She can't be. I should give him another blue pill and stop this, right now! But everything's gotten so out of control. If I just wait 'til someone says something real; something that actually makes sense; something believable—

"My *brother*," says Gran, "is so toxic, it's a wonder we're even related."

"Much younger, *half*-brother," Aldon says. "And *you're* the toxic half."

"Stop it," I yell, grabbing Gran's arm. "Why are you all lying? Our family are good, honest people. Not greedy, selfish Conqips." Gran looks at me, stunned, and shrugs her shoulders. "What about everything you said about sugar, and not caring about money, and—"

Aldon sniggers. "Your sweet granny can't get enough of it. What do you think she was doing in Switzerland?" Why would Gran have warned us about the stolen billions in the letter she sent if she was in on it and stealing the money herself? No, it's all lies. It has to be.

"Come, Monzi, and girl," says Gran. "We have to do something about Isaac before it's too late."

I step back and she turns to Moojag, but he hovers away from her, too. Hmm. She's forgotten me again, but she hasn't had an MP for a while. "Not 'til you explain what you're doing here," I say, even though she probably wouldn't remember. "And why you lied to everyone."

"I never lie," she says. "You mustn't believe a word Aldon says. He's always trying to turn people against each other. It's what he does. I ought to just leave him here in the sticky mess he created for himself."

Aldon grins, shaking his head. "No skin off my back."

My skin. "I'll have that PIE back now," I say, crossing my arms.

He raises his brow at me and mutters, "With pleasure. Horrid bit of technology, anyway." He takes off my PIE and chucks it to the side.

Moojag returns it to me with a bow and watches as I pull it up over the nightie. "Ward?" he asks.

I nod and jump up, relieved to finally be back in my own skin. "Okay," I say, handing Moojag the last pills and the pineapple. "We'd better take *uncle* with us, too."

Moojag nods, hauling Aldon and tucking him under his arm like a pre-Surge yoga mat, as I scoop up Gran and lay her across my shoulders. We leap off the stage and sprint down the aisle, straight out through the open theatre doors.

20

ISAAC

"So why *did* you go to Switzerland?" I ask Gran, as we charge out of Stikleby Hall.

"We had a tip-off about Isaac—that he was involved in the stolen billions."

"So you went to Switzerland for the money?"

"We didn't care about the money. We just wanted to find Stella's boy. But when we discovered the money had funded a underground bunker, and a bunch of weapons, too, we knew Isaac would be there with them. And that's when I realised they were all here under the lighthouse!"

"And Monzi, too," I say, stalling on the candy path with Moojag.

"Right," says Gran.

"So you didn't come down here to steal artificial

candy, then?"

Gran chuckles. "Of course not. Isn't life sweet enough as it is, in our Real World?" I nod. Aldon grunts like a pig. Moojag rattles him quiet as we turn the corner and enter the Ward.

"What's this?" calls Brix, glaring at Gran and Aldon as we plant them down next to each other on the floor. "Joined the sad Wrinkly Bones, now, have we, A'?"

"I should have known you were up to no good, Blockhead," says Aldon.

"You've always been a weak leader," says Brix. "Everyone agrees. It's high time for a fresh face around here."

"Not *your* ugly mug, surely," mutters Aldon.

"Seen yourself in the mirror lately?" asks Brix.

"Couldn't if I wanted to. Your pasty zit of a face is plastered to it thirty-four hours a day."

Brix steps over and kicks him in the shin. I step between them as uncle Aldon lifts his knees up to his chest.

"And what are *you* still doing here?" Brix yells directly at me. "Real World nerd back for her Franco-mute boyfriend, eh?"

"He's my brother!"

"Get your stupid, nerdy, wrinkly family away from me," he says, shaking his head. "Just go back to your pathetic *unconscious* community, where you belong. While you still have one!"

"You won't get your dirty hands on the Real World," I say, stepping forward to jab his shoulder but give it a pathetic poke instead.

"*Ugh,*" he says with a groan, pretending to jab me back in the chest. "I wouldn't touch that cesspit of an island if it was the last place on earth."

"I don't think you have much choice, love," says Stella, tapping him on the shoulder. "Do you?"

"What are you twittering on about now, idiot," he says, laughing in their face and flicking them on the chin.

I shake my head. I wish I still had a mum. What could Stella, or Brix's dad, have done to him to make him talk to them like that? Or maybe he even came out of them talking that way!

No such thing as a perfect parent, Nem. But Stella loves that boy more than anything in the whole wide wonderfully imperfect world.

Wait, who was that? I sniff the air as it fills with the scent of… honeysuckle. Mum?

"It's okay, dear," says Sophia, stroking Brix's shoulder. He jerks her hand away. "Whatever it is that's bothering you, just get it off your chest. We're here, now."

"We came down for you," says Stella. "To bring you back home. Whatever you've done, or whatever you're planning, it doesn't have to be."

"Home?" he says, laughing. "'Home' is where I'm left in peace to do what I want, surrounded by *normal* people."

Hmm. He'd be alone, then. A real nowhere man. Because there are no *normal* people. I wonder what our friend Wats would have made of all this. Where is he now, when we could really use his help? He always seems to turn up out of somewhere, whenever we're in a sticky situation, fixing it with his wonderfully strange words that somehow make perfect sense.

Brix stamps his foot and barges past us to poke his head out into the corridor. "Come on!" he hollers. Eight Conqips march straight in after him. "Escort them all to Porto Gajoom and shoot them out to you-know-where so we can get on with you-know-what." The Conqips heave Aldon and Gran up into their arms and shuttle us all out of the Ward. "But wait there, this time!" he yells at the men. "Be sure they don't come back down."

Don't worry, my love, everything will be okay. Just trust your intuition—and your brother!

Mum? Is that really you?

Moojag glances back. Did he hear her, too? He winks, but not at me. I turn around. Nothing but the Conqip following us. The expressionless man pushes me on ahead. I stumble forward and walk up alongside my brother. Our super senses are *seriously* working overtime today.

EXOPOF

The Conqips march us through the tunnel for the Switching Room and release the door.

I turn to Moojag as the men step inside and lay Gran and uncle Aldon down on the floor. "Where's Deja?" I whisper. He winks, pressing a finger to his lips, and points up. The entire ceiling is covered in a huge cloud of frozen-still, curled-up Pofs. It's like a gigantic flying-flower-saucer with multi-colored petals and its yellow pistil—Deja—at its centre. The grinning Pof spies Moojag and the pineapple and watches it like a hawk. The Conqips are too busy guarding the doors to spot the unusually silent swarm of Pofs overhead.

Dad said pre-Surgers almost never listened or

Mum? Is that really you?

Moojag glances back. Did he hear her, too? He winks, but not at me. I turn around. Nothing but the Conqip following us. The expressionless man pushes me on ahead. I stumble forward and walk up alongside my brother. Our super senses are *seriously* working overtime today.

EXOPOF

The Conqips march us through the tunnel for the Switching Room and release the door.

I turn to Moojag as the men step inside and lay Gran and uncle Aldon down on the floor. "Where's Deja?" I whisper. He winks, pressing a finger to his lips, and points up. The entire ceiling is covered in a huge cloud of frozen-still, curled-up Pofs. It's like a gigantic flying-flower-saucer with multi-colored petals and its yellow pistil—Deja—at its centre. The grinning Pof spies Moojag and the pineapple and watches it like a hawk. The Conqips are too busy guarding the doors to spot the unusually silent swarm of Pofs overhead.

Dad said pre-Surgers almost never listened or

looked up. He said they 'missed out on life's most beautiful sounds and sights' because of it.

Wendy Pof, sat cross-legged in the middle of the room with a pre-Surge tablet, grins up at the Conqip standing beside her. "Yes, please, how can I help, Sir?"

"We're sending them back," he says. "Open the gate to Porto Gajoom, at once."

Wendy bolts up and sticks out her hand. The Conqip pulls a chocolate brownie square from his pocket and stuffs it in her mouth. She nods, cheeks bulging, and skips over to door PG. "Aldon, too?" she mumbles, squinting back.

"All of them. And they're not to return." He leans over and whispers something in her ear.

"Okay, young man," she says, wiping the door down with a red cloth and pulling it open. She steps away, revealing the galley between us and the throbbing pink marshmallow wall. The Conqip orders Stella and Sophia to leave first.

But Deja will move the moment that precious pineapple does. So we have to get all the Pofs out with her now, or they'll never leave. I poke Moojag and jerk my head in the direction of the unmanned WC door behind us. He nods and sneaks the pineapple from inside his waistcoat.

Checking that Deja is looking, he quickly passes the fruit to Sophia, before taking my hand, and we make a dash for it.

"Stop, right there!" one of the Conqips call out, as they all charge after us for WC.

I glance back from the doorway, through the suits, and catch a glimpse of Deja diving into the marshmallow after the grannies, followed by all the Pofs, all at once! Two Conqips turn back to throw Gran and Aldon in, just as the tip of Wendy's scarlet wing is sucked last through the marshmallow.

I jump into WC, slamming the door in the Conqips' faces, and join Moojag hiding behind the giant toilet bowl. He hovers up onto the loo's rim and tips his hat. "Meet you on the upside," he says, jumping feet first into the swirling water as the door swings open. Moojag, why did you have to go back in! I bet he's gone looking for our dead mother.

The Conqip men charge up to the toilet bowl and split into two groups, marching round either side of the bowl. "IF," I whisper into Spondylux, just as one spots me.

"Huh? Where'd she go?" he cries, about to grab my arm. I sneak past him and dodge between them all, to creep back into the Switching Room.

There's someone laying there, in the middle of the abandoned hexagonal space. Gran! "Why are you back?" I ask.

"Who's that?" she calls, craning her neck.

"It's me, Nema," I say, patting her shoulder.

She flinches and grabs my hand. "Little Nema? But where? I can't see you—"

"What's Wrinkly Bones One still doing here?" shouts Travis, charging straight for us.

"Release Zoe at once!" yells Gran.

"You daft old bat," he says, tutting. "Not been taking your MPs again. Hmm?"

I crouch down to tickle him behind the knee. "Get off," he says, snorting as he tries desperately not to laugh. "Get this woman off me, PDQ!" Pretty Damn Quick.

Another Conqip runs in, frowning at him. "There's no one *on* you, Trav'?"

"There!" he says pointing to Gran lying curled up on the floor.

The Conqip laughs at him. "That old bat? The woman can barely move."

"But that *old bat* just tickled my leg!"

"Pulled your leg, more like."

I scoop up Gran and make for the Marshmallow Wall. "Put me down, you nasty Conqip!"

"It's only me," I whisper.

I hook my arms under hers and haul us backwards into the deep pink gunk. The men gawk at each other, then back at Gran being magically sucked through the pink wall. But she's only made it halfway through. Just her upper body is sticking out of the white wall on the other side with me.

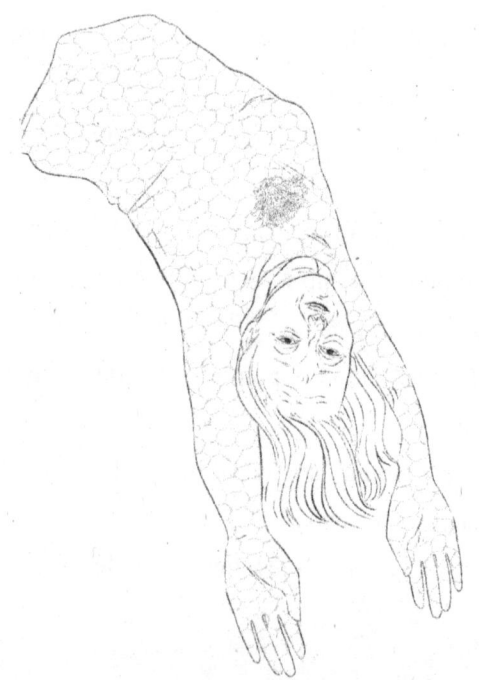

I tug harder, but she isn't budging: the Conqips must be pulling *her* leg now.

"A little help from your friends?" calls a familiar Scottish voice, making me jump and Gran wobble in the squidgy white wall. "Only half a granny, I see—"

I whisper "IF off," into Spondylux and glance back at Wats. "Help," I call, holding on tight to Gran's arms. "Grab my middle and pull, on 'go'!"

He skips over and wraps his arms around me. "Sure. Wouldn't want to be stuck in a strawberry field forever!"

"Ready, steady—"

"All together now!"

Gran flops out with a pop, as we bounce back onto the floor.

"Who is this?" asks Gran, glaring at the stunned fellow.

"Wats, at your service, Ma'am."

"Take me back."

"Sure thing, honey. The Real World is awaiting on you. Back to where you once belonged!"

"No," she says, stamping her fist on the ground. "Back in *there*, where I just came from!"

"But we have to leave, Gran," I explain.

"Who's the girl?" she asks Wats.

"Hmm. Let me see," he says, eyeing me up and down, before rolling me over. "Long Tall Sally? Mae… be Maggie, or dear Prudence, perhaps? Not dizzy Miss Izzy, for she has already come out to play—"

"It's me, Nema," I add, with a smile.

He strokes my arm and turns to Gran. "Or could it be polythene Pam? For she too is covered in silky fashions!"

"She just told you she's Nema."

"Of course she is," he says, grabbing my hand and shaking it firmly. "I'd have gotten you in the end!"

"Take me back," Gran says, pointing at the now solid white wall.

"It's too dangerous, Gran."

"Must you keep calling me 'Gran'?"

"We have to get back to the Real World, Nem Avti."

"But they've got Zoe," she whimpers. "We have to get her out, before it's too late!"

If only Mum *was* here. I take her hand in mine and sigh. "What now, Wats?"

"Of course. *Always* Wats!"

I whisper in his ear, "I *mean*, how do we get her home? And Moojag's gone back down again."

He shakes his head. "Let it be. A Moojag's gotta do what a Moojag's gotta do."

Wats is right. I've tried to get Moojag out twice, now. And it's too dangerous to turn back. "Zoe's gone, Nem Avti. We need to go home."

"You're sure she's safe?" asks Gran.

I nod and turn to Wats as an arch appears in the vibrating white wall. It could be Moojag coming through, but it's probably the Conqips. "Let it be, lady," Wats says, dragging Gran to the centre of the massive, white, circular, domed room.

THE BOMB

I sit Gran up inside the column of brilliant light at the centre of the vast white space. "Am I in heaven?" she asks, gazing round.

Wats giggles, dancing a little highland jig. "'Tis indeed a stairway to heaven!"

"We're in Porto Gajoom, Nem Avti," I say, pointing up to the big, perfectly round hole in the ceiling. "We shoot through that oculus to get home."

"Home," she says, bowing her head. "Will Mother be there?"

"Deidre?" I ask.

Gran nods. "Is she well?"

I don't want to lie, but I don't want to break her

heart, either. To discover her mum died over twenty years ago, and that she's forgotten it, too. "She's well." Gran looks relieved, but not as much as I feel.

Wats leaps up and depresses the circular pad on the floor with his foot, to release two transparent shafts from above. One from the oculus, and the other, from a new hole that's opened up in the left side of the dome ceiling. A red light flashes as they hover down at once, interlinking and stopping just above our heads. "I've got a feeling," says Wats, "it's *this* one."

Last time we left Gajoomdom, there was only *one* chute. Now there's two, and they're so twisted round each other that you can't see which one ends up at the oculus! I shake my head and glance back at the arched bit of wall we just came out of. It's pulsating again, with two pairs of white hands now pushing through it. "Out of time! The right one? *You* pick!"

Wats skips round the left chute. "Loves me," he says, jumping to the right one, "loves me not," to the left one, "loves me," to the right, "loves me not," to the left, "loves me. The left one!" he says, finally. He hugs the transparent tube and plants a big sloppy kiss on it.

We shove Gran under the chute and huddle in beside her. A blast of air lifts us off the floor and shuttles us halfway up. I look back down at the wall and Brix and Travis' white bodies protruding from it like rubber moulds. The shaft jolts, bends to the left, and another blast of air flies us like a bullet train toward the other hole opening in the side of the roof: the *wrong* one!

"The end, baby," calls Wats, as we fly out and hover for a moment before being plopped out onto a cold, shiny tiled floor. The dimmed space has a single thin slice of a window. Is this the lighthouse? I only ever saw the steps outside of it, before we ate Izzy's glykoriza rolls and then woke up underground in Gajoomdom. *Blue* glykoriza. "Here comes the sun, *dooo, doo, dooo, doo*…" chants Wats, leaping up and skipping over to a pair of glistening gold double doors. The wall isn't curved like the inside of a lighthouse, though. And there are four walls and four corners... This is a cement box!... Are we at London Tops? Wats battles with a big sliding lock chain before finally swinging the doors open and stumbling out.

"Are we home, Zoe?" Gran asks me.

I shade her eyes from the brilliant sunlight. "You

should wear this," I say, pointing to my PIE.

"Not mine," she says, shaking her head.

"Just 'til we get you yours back."

I take it off and pull it onto her feet. She lifts her bottom so I can stretch it up over her body, and I pull the sleeves up her arms as she wriggles her spindly fingers into the glove ends.

"Straight to the shelter, Zoe," she says, as we jump up together. "We'll tell them the wonderful news about PIE!"

I hold her hand and we step outside—hopefully onto Juniper Top and *not* a London Top. I pinch my nostrils closed from a strange toxic odour in the air, that smells of burning plastic, and look back at the building. It's a gold-covered skyscraper, shaped like a champagne bottle, towering over us with a long plume of dirty grey smoke billowing from its funneled roof. There's not a single other human or animal in sight: just a wide stretch of dry land surrounded by water. I turn round and spot another island in the distance with a tiny lighthouse and a mini Myrta ship moored up beside it. *That's* Juniper Top!

"Free as a bird," says Wats, pointing to a third island in the other direction, with a tiny curved wall at its edge.

The viewpoint on Box Hill! But if this isn't Juniper, Box Hill, *or* London Tops… where *are* we? I shake my head and lean in to the Spondylux on Gran's chest to *whatsnapchatinstatwitface* Dad, when the sound of footsteps and a man screaming about unlocked doors echoes out from the building. We run round the side to hide as two men stumble out laughing uncontrollably.

"Now that stupid old Aldon and all the feather-brained nerds are gone, I'm finally free to get on with my glorious plan!"

BRIX.

"*Our* plan," says the other one.

I peek round. It's Travis, combing his hair into one of his ever tinier quiffs.

"The measly Real World deserves them," says Brix. "For now, at least."

"It's fun being in charge!" says Travis, with a smirk.

"Yes, well, try not to forget who's in charge of *you*."

"When do we deliver our big bad *bomb*, Boss?"

"Patience," says Brix, muting Travis with his hand. "First we have to sort Aldon's dump."

Travis chuckles. "I love it when we destroy stuff.

None of that fix-it nonsense and 'recycle, upcycle' business. Absolute rubbish."

"Well, precisely."

"Except," mutters Travis, "what about Buzby and the Loon?"

"Shut up and go fetch that beautiful thing."

Travis trudges back into the building and comes out dragging a rectangular white metal sheet with two long square leg poles attached to the bottom of it. We shuffle further back round the corner as they lug the ugly thing across a freshly tarmacked black path and over to the hill's edge. They plant it firmly into two deep holes in the ground, hi-five each other, and turn back for the building, cackles fading as they disappear inside. The doors close and the chain clinks, sliding back into place.

"What *is* that thing?" I whisper to Wats.

"You're not going to like it," says Gran.

I turn back to spy through the slit window, checking that the Conqips have definitely gone, and we creep over to the *thing*.

It's a big sign with angry red letters, that reads:

Welcome to the
ISLE OF BRIX
NO ENTRY TO REAL WORLDERS, **EVER!!!**

(NO PIEs, NO greens, NO fruit, NO purified water, NO dogs,
OR cats, NO do-gooders, NO sharing, NO rights, NO thinking,
NO feather-brained inventions, NO exercise, NO breathing fresh air)

*Healthy visitors will be held in solitary confinement for minimum one year, unless a compulsory donation of one thousand bottles of champagne is made to President BRIX on arrival.

23

PEACE GAJOOM

"No *breathing*!?" I shout, squeezing Gran's arm.

"They aren't fans of the outdoors," she explains.

"They aren't fans of *living*," I say, brows raised. "Why on earth would you keep healthy people locked up in that bottle for a year?"

"Personally, I wouldn't choose to stay here in the first place," says Gran. "But we've far more important things to think about, now, darling."

"What things?"

"Who is this clueless girl?" Gran asks Wats. "Where has Nema gone?"

"She definitely isn't polythene Pam," answers Wats, scratching his chin. "And, as I said, Dizzy's back in RW."

I huff. "It's me, *I'm* Nema—your granddaughter."

Gran laughs, shaking her head, and rests a hand on Wats' shoulder. "Did you bring the little peacekeepers, Man?"

"Sure thing," he answers, pointing to a mound of loose soil behind 'Champagne Building'. "All aboard." I follow them over to the suspicious pile of rubble that seems to be moving. Something's alive in there! Wats digs an arm in and pulls out a wriggling thing. A mini Gajoom! But it has a silver stripe, not a purple one, spiraled round it.

Gran *has* been stealing from Aldon! "So Uncle *was* telling the truth," I say, scowling at her and crossing my arms. "And you both knew about this place?"

"Who's your uncle, darling?"

"Aldon! Your brother? He *is* your brother, isn't he? Or did you lie about that, too?" I don't feel like myself any more, talking like this. I don't recognise Gran either, right now.

"Zoe," she says, "don't despair. You're free now! And it's time to put our plan in action, before Blockhead sets off his B."

"B?" I ask, shaking my head.

"Bomb," whispers Wats in my ear. The 'big' and 'bad' thing Travis was talking about? What are they all up to!?

"Wats!" cries Gran, tutting at him. "We don't say the B word any more."

Wats salutes her and places the Gajoom, who was all cosy, curled up in his arm, back down on the ground. Gran pokes them and says, "IF, ickle Gajoom!"

The stick of rock rubs its head—yes, its top end—against Wats' leg and disappears into thin air. Oh, that's just *great*. There are still angry Gajooms, and now they've got the IF, too!

"Aldon was right," says Gran. "I *was* stealing. But I wasn't stealing artificial sweets *or* eating them! I was collecting baby Gajooms to create our very own Gajoom *peace* army! These," she says, unearthing another nine sticks from the mound, "are our dream 'super tech Gajooms'."

Okay. I sigh with relief. These are *good* Gajooms.

"Yes, darling," she says, with a grin. "Another one of your bright ideas!"

"My idea?"

"Don't fret, love. It will all come back to you."

"But why do we need a peace army, if we got rid of the nasty code on all the Gajooms and there isn't going to be any war?"

"The B, darling," whispers Gran. "And I never want to hear the W word pass from your lips, ever again!"

"What *is* a B!?" I yell back at her. She glares at me like I actually bit off the top of her head. But I didn't *mean* to shout—it was like something made me do it. What must she think of me? At least she thinks I'm Mum right now, and not Nema.

"Big explosion," says Wats, digging his hands into his hips. "No more Box Hill! Bang, bang, *pooooof*."

"You *know*," says Gran, "those nasty things that used to blow up entire countries and populations—"

"What! But why would Brix want to blow us up? I know the Conqip don't like the Real World, but—"

"They don't like us, of course," agrees Gran, "but it's worse than that. We think they discovered gas under Box Hill. There was talk about it before the Surge, and then we came along and must have ruined their great big plans."

"But isn't that what they were doing before the Resource Wars, when they ran out of oil?"

Gran nods. "Exactly, and it's happening all over again." Spondylux vibrates as a *whatsnapchatinstatwitface* loads, and she stands back to let it project its holograph out in front of us. A tall man with shoulder-length, wavy brown hair, wearing a sparkling white PIE, comes into focus.

"Dad!"

"Nema, love!"

"Dad, we're in so much trouble," I say, burying my head in my chest.

"No fear—we're on our way," he says. "We're coming down to get you both right now!" Wait—he thinks we're still in Gajoomdom.

"Nem Avti, is that you?" he asks.

"It is she," answers Gran. "Who is asking?"

"It's me, Jack."

"My Jack?"

"Yes. Are you okay, Mother? Stella and Sophia told us everything. Well, at least what they could remember—"

"But we're not in Gajoomdom any more, Dad," I say, turning Gran and the Spondylux round. "We can see Juniper Top from here, and the Myrta, but everything looks tiny!"

Dad turns to speak to someone behind him and then looks back. "I'm not sure if we're imagining this, love," he says, pouting, "but we can see an island with a gargantuan bottle standing on top of it—"

"Yes! That's here, where *we* are!" I show him the smoking building behind us. "It's a skyscraper, shaped like a champagne bottle. We think the Conqip are going to blow up Box Hill!"

"Are they now?" he says, screwing up his forehead, as a grumpy old man grunts behind him. "Hold tight and don't move. We should make it there in approximately… Captain? What do you say—five nautical miles?"

"To be sure," replies our glitter-bearded fisher friend Phil, appearing at the helm. "Full speed ahead!"

Five nautical miles? That will take them at least twenty minutes at full speed.

"Right, we're on our way!" says Dad. "Just remember: don't worry—and be happy! Good *always* overcomes in the end, you know…"

I don't think you're right, this time, though, Dad. What good can come from a blown up Real World? That's worse than any bad stuff we could ever imagine.

We'd have to leave Box Hill forever... Worse—we could all end up dead!

24

BOMBSENSE

Gran taps my shoulder as the *whatsnapchatinstatwitface* with Dad fizzles out. "Shall we?" she says, turning my head to see the little silver-striped Gajooms all lined up like soldiers in a neat row. "Time for the hunt! Our Peace Gajooms can detect weapons, with their five hundred million olfactory receptor cells." That's five times a dog's smelling power! And something like a hundred more than ours. I bend down to inspect one. It wiggles, rubbing itself against my arm, then plucks its sticky, sugary self clean away, leaving not a single trace of candy. "Thanks to chemist Isiah Warner's marvellous electronic nose!" Gran continues. "Dear Peace Gajooms," she tells all the sticks, "go detect the B!"

"Come on, my Michelle," says Wats, hopping after

them.

"Wait!" I call, "Dad said not to move—"

"Chop chop," calls Gran. "We'll be back well before he gets here. The Gajooms are super efficient!"

The eager sticks leap forward and bolt off round the building, with Gran and Wats skipping behind. As I chase after them, my nose gets a strange whiff of something. Banana? The sticks bow down sniffing the ground and hop a few metres further along to a small square patch of ground covered with loose soil. Wats dusts it away to reveal a large wooden hatch.

"Anyone else smell bananas?" I ask.

Gran nods. "Oh my, yes indeed."

"But there aren't any," I say, scanning round. There isn't a banana tree or even a single banana in sight. A Gajoom spins in front of me and stomps excitedly. "What do they want?"

"I believe," says Wats, "they're agreeing with you!"

"Nitroglycerin," exclaims Gran. "It smells like banana! Sobrero invented the stuff in 1846. Two hundred years ago. I bet this is a big one."

"A big *what*? Bomb?"

"B, girl, *B*," she hisses, pointing at the hatch.

I must have that super sense the Auts' carer, Charlie, was talking about before we all escaped with them for the Real World! She said the Auts' senses were so overwhelming that they were too afraid to use them. Charlie must be the scientist who was at the clinic when the Conqip snatched them all. Gran must have this super sense, too, if she can smell the nitro-thingy as well! "Are you an Aut?" I ask her.

She smiles and winks back. "Aren't we all?"

"No. Not all people are Aut. I don't think the Conqips are Auts. Unless *everyone* can smell Bs buried underground. *Can* they?" But maybe not *all* Auts can smell Bs.

Gran nods. "True. Not an easy superpower to live with, darling. Smells can be glorious, but very often overbearing. For hunting, though, most useful indeed!"

"I didn't know I had that ability. I know we're all different, but I never even knew I was an Aut!"

"Well, why would you. After all, it's quite normal for us RWs, being us."

Wats shakes his head. "I can't smell said banana. But I haven't smelled a thing since 2021."

"I'm sorry," I say. Poor Wats, not being able to smell.

What must that be like? To have forgotten the beautiful scent of flowers, and not be able to tell any more when food is still fresh, or when the weather's turning.

"It's been a hard day's night," says Wats, "but no fear, I have my other wonderful senses, to make up for the lack of me nozzle." He strokes the Gajooms and ushers them out of the way while Gran and I bend down to pull up the hatch. How many olfactory cells must Gran and I have? Not nearly as many as these Gajooms, that's for sure. She'll have at least doubled the number for their sensory code.

"Nobel's dynamite, Zoe," says Gran, peering into the hole. "Ironic, really. Giving out a peace prize when you've designed a weapon of W. They said Nobel's brother died from an explosion in the factory when he was helping him develop the stuff. The guy did give away all the money he made from it, though. At least, that's what they told everyone. Not what a Conqip would have done, *oh no*."

Dynamite. Like *dynami*. "From the Greek word for power and strength?" I ask.

"Indeed. Pure physical power. Strong enough to blow up a building or an island from the inside out. If you have enough of it, that is."

I look down into the deep hole. Inside, lies a giant taped-up bundle of at least one hundred purple and white striped sticks. The dynamite looks like a bunch of Gajoomstiks! A big, digital clock displaying six zeros is tied around the top, and a long, black plastic cord snakes around it. The Gajooms creep forward and bolt straight back.

"How rude," I say, "making the dynamite look like Gajooms!" Can the Gajooms see, though? Because they definitely don't have eyes. Maybe they can *smell* the shape of the stripes around the sticks?

"Typical Conqip behaviour," says Gran, gently patting the trembling Gajoom cowering behind her. "Now, what to do about this horrendous stuff?"

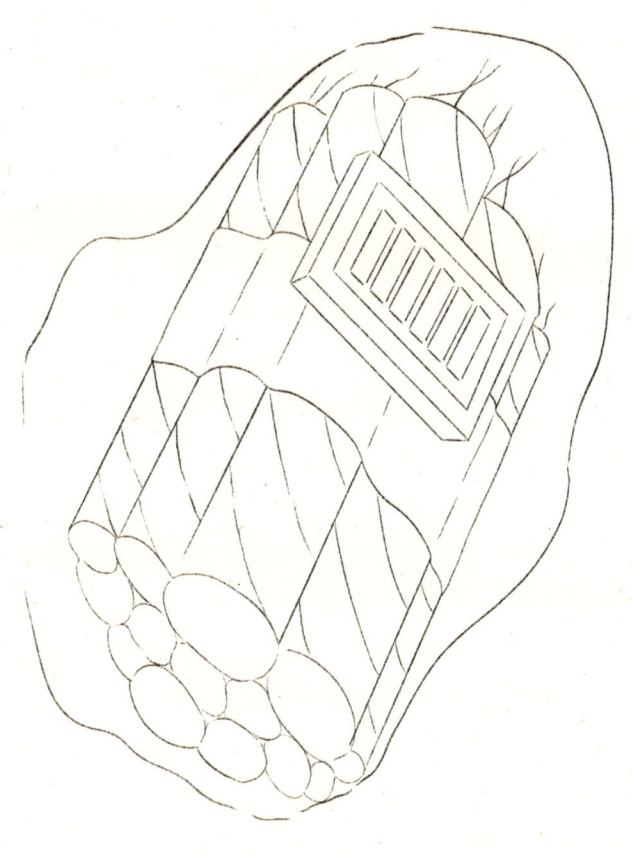

HONEYSUCKLE

"Is it dangerous?" I ask, stepping back beside the little Peace Gajooms.

"Only when the cord is lit," answers Gran, with a rattling sound coming from the building. It's the door chain sliding out of its lock!

Wats presses a finger to his lips and ushers us and the Gajooms over to a thick, old oak, a few feet away. The only tree that seems to be left standing on this sad island. I wonder why they didn't just chop this one down, too?

The doors swing open and a human-sized Gajoom bounds out along with a man's voice calling, "Nema? Where are you?" It's coming from the Gajoom!

"Monty?" calls Wats, jumping out from behind the tree.

"Yes, it's me, Biermont," answers our friendly ex-Conqip, catching his breath as he pulls off the disguise. "We have a little problem."

"Who's *this* guy, now?" asks Gran, squinting at him suspiciously.

"Biermont," he answers. "The *good* Conqip."

Gran laughs in his face. "Good?" she says, turning to Wats. "Pretending to be something he's not?"

"He *is* good," I say. "You can trust him."

"Not important," says Biermont, glancing back at the building. "It's Moojag. He's stuck in the Ward."

"Stuck?" I ask.

"Brix caught him and locked him in with the woman."

"What woman?" I never saw a single woman down there, other than Charlie. And she's back safe in RW now. Or..?

"Who's Moojag?" asks Gran.

"Your grandson, Monzi," I answer.

She looks up for a moment, then glares back at me. "We must hurry—the Zizanth have Monzi!"

"They did have him, but that was before. The

Conqip have him now, and there's some woman trapped down there with him, too."

"I believe this Beer Man," says Gran. "He speaks the truth." She clenches her fist in the air. "The woman is Zoe, I tell you. They've got Zoe!"

I shake my head. "Did you know about this place, too?" I ask Biermont. "And the dynamite?"

"Afraid so. Not about the dynamite, though. That must be a recent development."

"Brix is planning to blow up the Real World!" I say.

"I don't know about that," says Biermont, "but he's definitely going to blow up Gajoomdom, and he's going to do it *now*. I just heard him ordering Travis to set it off in twenty minutes!"

"What? But Moojag! And all the Gajooms, too. We have to get rid of it," I say, pointing to the pit full of *dynami*.

"I'm afraid that isn't the stuff they're going to use," he adds. "There's a super bomb." Gran's eyes widen. Is she more shocked about the word 'BOMB' right now, or the actual BOMB? "Only Brix and Travis know where it is," continues Biermont. "And they've finally found me out, so I couldn't get the key for the Ward. Well, I was lucky to

"Yes, it's me, Biermont," answers our friendly ex-Conqip, catching his breath as he pulls off the disguise. "We have a little problem."

"Who's *this* guy, now?" asks Gran, squinting at him suspiciously.

"Biermont," he answers. "The *good* Conqip."

Gran laughs in his face. "Good?" she says, turning to Wats. "Pretending to be something he's not?"

"He *is* good," I say. "You can trust him."

"Not important," says Biermont, glancing back at the building. "It's Moojag. He's stuck in the Ward."

"Stuck?" I ask.

"Brix caught him and locked him in with the woman."

"What woman?" I never saw a single woman down there, other than Charlie. And she's back safe in RW now. Or..?

"Who's Moojag?" asks Gran.

"Your grandson, Monzi," I answer.

She looks up for a moment, then glares back at me. "We must hurry—the Zizanth have Monzi!"

"They did have him, but that was before. The

Conqip have him now, and there's some woman trapped down there with him, too."

"I believe this Beer Man," says Gran. "He speaks the truth." She clenches her fist in the air. "The woman is Zoe, I tell you. They've got Zoe!"

I shake my head. "Did you know about this place, too?" I ask Biermont. "And the dynamite?"

"Afraid so. Not about the dynamite, though. That must be a recent development."

"Brix is planning to blow up the Real World!" I say.

"I don't know about that," says Biermont, "but he's definitely going to blow up Gajoomdom, and he's going to do it *now*. I just heard him ordering Travis to set it off in twenty minutes!"

"What? But Moojag! And all the Gajooms, too. We have to get rid of it," I say, pointing to the pit full of *dynami*.

"I'm afraid that isn't the stuff they're going to use," he adds. "There's a super bomb." Gran's eyes widen. Is she more shocked about the word 'BOMB' right now, or the actual BOMB? "Only Brix and Travis know where it is," continues Biermont. "And they've finally found me out, so I couldn't get the key for the Ward. Well, I was lucky to get away—"

"We're going back in!" calls Gran, leaping forward. "Wats: you and Beer Man wait here for Jack. And hunt down any more Bs, while you're at it."

"Okay," agrees Wats, "but *whatsnapchatinstatwitface*, and get back quick!"

"Will do," answers Gran.

Why did my brother have to stay down there again? And all this stuff with Mum, thinking she's alive. Why couldn't he just let it go? Is Charlie the woman with him? Because she wasn't in the hologram with Dad. Did she come back down after me, to help rescue Moojag, and get caught?

We race back to the building, crawl under the chute, and wait for the air to blast us down through the floor, then across to Juniper Top, and back down into Porto Gajoom. We wade through the marshmallow wall and pop out into the Switching Room. I freeze as a thick scent of honeysuckle, with a dash of liquorice, hits me in the face, and a voice whispers,

Your brother is in danger. He needs you. Hurry!

I shake my head. I can't tell Gran I'm hearing Mum. She wouldn't understand, and it might confuse her even more.

"IF," she whispers, picking a door. "I'll just nip in and get that key, Nema."

"But—"

"No, you wait here."

The door clicks shut behind her. Please, *please* hurry, Gran. Why didn't we bring Peace Gajooms? I guess we won't have time to stop the B going off, even if we do find it. I peer into the factory at all the Gajooms. They're neatly lined up in pairs beside the wall, as though they know what's happening. Is Brix taking them with him?

Hurry, my love!

Mum?

Told you I'd find her, Sis!

"Moojag?" I call, spinning round. "Where are you, I can't see you?"

We're in the Auticode cell, at the palace.

How can I hear Moojag if he's in Pof Palace? What if the woman *is* Mum? That would mean all three of us have super sensory hearing, and she really *has* been talking to us this whole time. And it hasn't just been our sensory memories playing tricks!

The door slides open and Gran steps back in holding up a key. "We're out of time! Travis has already detonated the bomb and the Conqips are leaving Gajoomdom, *right now*." She sniffs the air and leans forward to sniff me, too. "Honeysuckle?"

I nod. "But it's not *me*. You were right! Zoe *is* the woman with Moojag. I'm really sorry for not believing you, Gran—"

"Of course! Only Zoe smells of honeysuckle. The scent's been right under my nose since the day I arrived in this dreadful place—"

"I know where they are," I say, sprinting for door T42, "and we won't need that key. Come on!"

We run out to Pof Palace, climb the stairs of the deserted building, cross the hall, crawl through the tunnel in the wall, and drop out into the same small dark space where Adam, Izzy, and I uncovered the Auticode.

Moojag is squatting in the corner of the room beside a huddled-up, frail woman with long black hair. They're squeezed between the cold, oily wall and a giant wooden crate box that almost takes up the entire room. It reeks of something toxic in here.

"Nema, is that you?" asks the woman, gazing up.

"Yes," I answer, dropping beside her and resting my head against her chest. "Mum?" I say, looking up at her face as she wraps her thin arms around me. She nods, stroking my hair. "But why didn't you tell us where you were?"

"I didn't know," she answers. "They brought me down here a very long time ago. I don't even know how much time it's been. Stuck in a dark room with only my memories of you and Monzi to keep me going. When I heard my boy," she says, glancing at Moojag, "I started talking to him. I didn't even know if he was real. And then when I heard the both of you, together, I knew it must be true. I've just been trying to keep you safe. I was afraid you'd all be angry with me for what happened to Monzi."

Gran lifts the lid of the giant box. "Looks like we've

found the great big ticking B. Ten minutes left on the timer, folks—ten minutes to get out of here!"

Travis must have been talking about Mum and Moojag when he asked Brix about 'Buzby and the Loon'. Which means Brix wants to kill them! He's a *lot* nastier than Aldon.

"Take good care of them for me," says Mum, gazing up at Gran. "I'd only slow you down." I shake my head.

"She can't walk," explains Moojag.

"Nonsense," says Gran, hands on hips. "Monzi: you take your mother; I'll carry the girl." She slings me over her shoulders and Zoe grabs on tight to Moojag's wings as he hauls her up.

They race us back to the switching room, where all six doors have been left wide open. There's no person or Gajoom in sight. Only an untouched, perfectly round and smooth chocolate orange sitting on the floor beside door PG. We wade through the marshmallow wall back into Porto Gajoom, and fly up the chute. But the tube doesn't bend—it just heads straight up and out, landing us in a room with a single curved wall.

The lighthouse!?

We've only gone and picked the wrong chute again, which means we're still at Juniper Top—over Gajoomdom, and on top of the BOMB!

"Are we home, dear?" asks Gran, peering around as we step outside.

"Not exactly," I say, pointing to a distant island with a humongous bottle on it, and a tiny shimmering rescue ship anchored in the harbour. "We're still on Juniper. Not the big bad Isle of Brix, where Dad is now."

Moojag glares at me. No time to explain. I shake my head.

"Fifty-five seconds," he exclaims, checking his smartwatch.

Well, as Dad would say, "There's never a bad time for a swim." We run down the path from the lighthouse to the water's edge, dodging all the little crustaceans scurrying for their lives—as if they know—and *whatsnapchatinstatwitface* Dad to tell him what's happened.

Gran kickboxes one of the mooring poles in the bay and heaves it out. "Zoe can hold on to this!"

"Why the stick," says Moojag, "when we have PIE?" I nod.

"Silly me," says Gran, chucking the pole over her shoulder and just missing a frazzled blue crab. She calls "PIE inflate!" into Spondylux and flops backwards into the water, flinging out her arms and legs as the e-skin puffs up all round her body and hood. Moojag and I roll Mum onto our granny lifeboat and push them out, when a gigantic explosion goes off. The whole island shakes from side to side and a huge current rushes through the water, whirling round our legs and spinning the boat around. A series of ear-splitting bangs vibrate and ring in our ears as a massive dust ball forms over the island, filling the sky with a great grey cloud. We cling on tight as a humongous wave grows up from the water and rolls away from the island, pushing us out to sea along with it. Frenzied fish and other sea creatures dart about, tickling our legs and feet. Behind us, over Juniper Top, glass shards and chunks of brick fly in all directions with the lighthouse collapsing and crumbling into a giant crater opening up beneath it.

A safe distance from the island, I look round at Moojag. He's pointing to the Myrta ship now turned in our direction. We climb onto Gran, either side of Mum, and bury our heads in her pillow-soft tum. The scent of honeysuckle

fills the air, as I gaze up at the very real, red-tinted sky. Gran wraps her inflated arms around us and looks down at me with a grin. "You see? I told you we'd all be together again, one day…"

Yes, Gran, you did, but you didn't tell me what you were doing with the Zizanth, and I am not going to let this go!

Have you listened to the full-cast audiobook, featuring Indica Watson and Ria Lina?

Download it now, from:
Audible - Amazon / GooglePlay / Apple / Kobo

Sketch your future tech inventions here... and share them with us:

@MOOJAGbook / info@moojag.com #MOOJAG #FutureTechInventors

Sketch your future tech inventions here... and share them with us:

@MOOJAGbook / info@moojag.com #MOOJAG #FutureTechInventors

LOVED MOOJAG?

Share your **MOOJAG** joy with us **@MOOJAGbook**
tagging **#MOOJAG #NDbooks #CliFi**
And post a review on the website of the
store where you bought your copy, or at:
*Amazon, Waterstones, Kobo,
Goodreads, TheStoryGraph, Toppsta*
and other book review sites.

**Subscribe to the Spondylux Press newsletter
for the chance of winning a free signed copy
and a stick of *real* GAJOOM ROCK CANDY!
Plus you'll get new release and events news too...**

www.moojag.com/newsletter.html